DEKOK AND THE
DEADLY ACCORD

DeKok and the Deadly Accord

by

BAANTJER

translated from the Dutch by H.G. Smittenaar

INTERCONTINENTAL PUBLISHING

ISBN 1 881164 14 4

Printing History:
　　　1st Dutch printing:　　1981
　　　17th Dutch printing　　1996

　　　1st American edition: 1996

Cover by: David Hendrickson and friends from the
　Cool Corpse Company in North Pole Alaska
Typography: Monica S. Rozier

Library of Congress Cataloging-in-Publication Data

Baantjer, A. C.
　　[De Cock en het dodelijke akkoord. English]
　　DeKok and the deadly accord / by Baantjer ; translated from the
Dutch by H.G. Smittenaar.
　　　　p.　　cm.
　　ISBN 1–881164–14–4 (pbk.) : $8.95
　　I. Smittenaar, H. G.
PT5881.12.A2C63813 1996
839.3'1364—dc21　　　　　　　　　　　　　　　　　96–36721
　　　　　　　　　　　　　　　　　　　　　　　　　　　　　　CIP

***DeKok
and the
Deadly Accord***

1

Jan-Willem Hoffman looked in amazement at the hand in front of him. The hand held a pistol and the barrel was aimed at Jan-Willem. In his imagination the scene was suddenly enlarged beyond measure. The enormous muzzle and beyond that the grooves and lands of the barrel seemed to fill his entire field of vision. With a small part of peripheral vision he saw the knuckles behind the barrel whiten. In a futile gesture he raised his hands as if to ward off the inevitable bullets. With the palms of his hands, the fingers widespread, he tried to stuff the bullets back into the barrel before they had been fired. Then the pistol spoke, spat fire . . . once, twice, thrice.

From a distance Jan-Willem felt his body react to the impact of the bullets. He felt them boring tunnels in his chest. With a grotesque movement he collapsed and fell on the fine gravel of the path. There was still a look of disbelief and utter astonishment on his gleaming, fat face. Then, he froze in death.

* * *

Detective-Inspector DeKok of the ancient, renowned police station at 48 Warmoes Street plodded along the Damrak, the busy street connecting Amsterdam's Central Station with Dam Square, considered by many to be the heart of Amsterdam.

DeKok's hands were buried deep inside the pockets of his old raincoat and his small, somewhat greasy, little hat barely covered his gray hair that escaped in large plucks from under the ridiculous headgear. His face, which usually showed the friendly expression of a good-natured boxer, looked grim and somber. His right hand emerged from his pocket, holding a toffee. He looked at it and then, with a grimace of distaste, put it back in his pocket.

Dick Vledder, DeKok's young friend, partner and assistant, walked next to the old man. He had noticed DeKok's movement with the toffee. A bad sign, he thought. The old man had a distinct sweet tooth and for him to pass up the opportunity to indulge it was almost unheard of. Vledder again looked at his mentor.

"Something bothering you?" he asked.

The gray sleuth did not answer. Vledder sighed. It was one of DeKok's many peculiarities that he could totally ignore a question as if it had never been asked. Depending on one's point of view, the habit could bring either chuckles of ironic laughter, or tears of frustration. But Vledder was used to DeKok's peculiarities and accepted them as another force of nature.

DeKok leaned deeper into the wind and at one point was forced to bring a hand up to his head to prevent his hat from being blown away. It was a strong wind, mixed with rain and sleet. Winter fought a furious rear-action battle against encroaching Spring.

They turned left near the Victoria Hotel. The wind seemed even stronger on Prince Henry Quay. Again DeKok had to make a quick grab for his hat as he cursed under his breath.

Vledder grinned broadly.

"Something *is* bothering you," he decided, almost jovially. "I see all the signs."

DeKok finally acknowledged his partner.

"Is there a law against it?" asked the old man grumpily.

Vledder shrugged his shoulders.

"You could start," he said calmly, "by explaining what's the matter. You've been walking around with a face like a thundercloud since early this morning and you growl and snarl at everybody who comes near. Poor Frans of Administration really got a piece of your mind."

DeKok grunted something unintelligible.

"What?" asked Vledder blandly.

"I'm sure," said DeKok, "that we've had dealings with Jan-Willem Hoffman at one time or another. Somehow I seem to remember that he came to Warmoes Street, some time ago. I just can't remember the connection."

"Come on, Frans searched all the files. He's not in our system. You must be mistaken."

DeKok shook his head, a determined look on his face.

"I'm not mistaken."

"But it's possible."

"Absolutely not," snorted DeKok. "I had a good look at the pictures taken of the corpse. I've seen that puffy face before. *That* I know for sure."

Vledder was confused.

"But why should you be interested. He was found on a gravel path in Rembrandt Park. That's a long way from the inner city. That's in the Sixth District and falls under the station in Deyssel Street. It's got nothing to do with us at Warmoes Street."

DeKok halted and with an irritated gesture planted his hat more firmly on his head.

"And it's got nothing to do with me," he said angrily. "And what's more, I don't *want* it to have anything to do with me."

He rubbed the bridge of his nose with a little finger. Then he looked at the finger for several seconds as if he had never seen it before. His face relaxed, his tone became milder.

"Jan-Willem Hoffman is, or rather . . . was, the son-in-law of Handy Henkie."

"The burglar?" Vledder was taken by surprise.

DeKok nodded slowly.

"The *ex*-burglar. Handy Henkie retired from the profession some years ago. He abandoned his criminal activities and now has become quite respectable. I may, I like to think, have had something to do with that. At the time I had a certain amount of influence on him. Since then he has not come to the attention of the police."

Vledder frowned.

"But Hoffman," he said hesitantly, "was Director of some kind of financial institution."

DeKok gave him a wan smile.

"And you are thinking: How come the daughter of a common criminal, a burglar, gets a man like that?"

"Yes."

"Josephine Haar was a good-looking and smart girl. And she used her head. After finishing High School, she enrolled in a Secretarial School. She became an Executive Secretary and in due course joined the bank."

"Where she met Hoffman."

"Exactly. Simple as that."

They walked on in silence. The wind increased and raged across the open waters of the harbor. Rain made visibility precarious.

Vledder finally broke the silence.

"Is Handy Henkie connected in some way?"

"With Hoffman's murder?"

"Yes."

DeKok made an impatient gesture.

"He came to visit me last night, at home. It was rather late in the evening. My wife and I were just about ready to go to bed. I

10

was dumbstruck when I found Henkie in front of my door. I hadn't seen him for years. He was upset, tense. So different from when I knew him. He told me about the marriage of his daughter and Jan-Willem Hoffman and asked me if I would take charge of the murder case. I tried to explain that it wasn't possible, that it was a case for the Sixth. He kept on urging me, however, and told me that he was worried about his daughter. What could I do? Eventually I agreed to speak to Josephine."

Vledder looked at his colleague and grinned softly to himself.

"I understand and now you're upset that you agreed."

DeKok waved his arms.

"I didn't really want to say 'no.' My inclination was to help Henkie, if for no other reason than sentimental reasons. In the past I've sent him up the river a number of times and although he undoubtedly deserved it, he lost a number of years of his life, thanks to me." He sighed elaborately. "On the other hand I don't feel like I want to be underfoot at Deyssel Street. They have their own worries." He paused and sighed again. "But, you see, I know full well what's bothering Henkie. He's afraid that during the investigation into Jan-Willem's murder, his own criminal past will come to light and that the gossip may harm his daughter."

"So."

"Just so. It is also not outside the realms of possibilities that Hoffman had difficulties of his own. After all, there must have been a reason for somebody to put three bullets in him."

The old cop stopped and looked up at the facade of Hotel-Restaurant *Beehive*. He walked toward the front door. Vledder rushed to catch up with him.

"Where are you going?"

DeKok half-turned.

"Josephine . . . I promised to meet her here."

* * *

They placed their wet raincoats on the coat rack and selected a table near the window. Vledder and DeKok came here often. When they did not eat in one of DeKok's favorite Indonesian restaurants, they would eat at the *Beehive*. The restaurant has a certain fame for its typical Dutch cuisine.

They ordered a cup of coffee and looked out. The wind chased the rain horizontally across the outside of the large plate glass windows. DeKok rubbed his hands and shivered.

"Not fit for man nor beast," he murmured. "Perhaps I would have been better off ordering a cognac."

"Well, have a cognac in your coffee," suggested Vledder.

"What?" DeKok's tone was horrified. "And dilute perfectly good cognac with a foreign substance?"

Suddenly there was a change in the old man's demeanor. There was a happy, surprised look on his face. Vledder turned around and saw a young woman approaching. A beautiful young woman with long, blonde hair down to her shoulders. She was dressed in a tight fitting suit of soft, black material which accentuated the exquisite lines of her figure.

DeKok almost did not recognize her. When he had last seen her, she was a teenager. She had been there when he had been forced to arrest her father. It had been a strange arrest, he recalled. Handy Henkie had cried like a child and Josephine, her face hard and uncompromising, had shown DeKok the place where her father had hidden the stolen fur coats. Slowly DeKok rose from his chair. With a smile on her lips, she extended a hand toward him.

"It's been a long time, Mr. DeKok." She tossed her head and her hair waved in the air around her. "I think I've changed a little, since then."

DeKok shook her hand.

"If I remember correctly, Josephine, you were seventeen at the time when you put paid to your father's brilliant career."

She wrinkled her nose.

"Some career," she said contemptuously.

DeKok did not react, but pointed in Vledder's direction.

"This is Dick Vledder, my esteemed colleague and friend."

She shook hands with Vledder and sat down at the table. The two men seated themselves across from her.

DeKok studied her. She had indeed grown up to become a beauty, he realized. She had a sweet, oval face with clear, blue eyes. There was just a hint of a certain hardness around the corners of her mouth. He pointed at the weather outside,

"You didn't get wet?"

She shook her head. Another, playful smile darted around the full mouth. It was a pleasant sight.

"I haven't been outside. After the death of my husband, I moved into this hotel. I'm afraid to go home."

"Why is that?"

She bit her lower lip.

"I don't know," she said. "There's no rational explanation for it. But after I was notified of his death, I haven't set foot in the house. I just can't make myself."

"Where do you live?"

"In Amstelveen, in the suburbs. About eight years ago we had a house built, there."

"Your husband is . . . was well off?"

She shrugged her shoulders.

"That's hard to say. It's all so sudden. I've been unable to find out what we have, what we own . . . or owe. Jan-Willem took care of all financial business. I never bothered with it."

"You married under community property laws?"

"Yes."

"Any children?"

13

"Two. A boy of seven and a girl of five years. Little darlings. For the time being they're staying with my in-laws."

DeKok gave her a sharp, observing look.

"The children will miss their father."

She pulled back slightly, an alert look in her eyes.

"They never saw much of their father. He was always too busy with business."

DeKok listened to the bitter tone. He also noticed how her face changed. The hard lines around her mouth became more prominent.

"Your husband," he asked in a friendly tone of voice, "did I ever meet him when he was still alive?"

She shrugged her shoulders and spread wide her hands.

"Not as far as I know. Perhaps without me knowing it?"

DeKok sipped his coffee.

"I saw his picture," he said with hesitation. "A police photo, shortly after he died." He paused and played with the spoon at the side of his cup. "I realize," he continued, "that somebody does not look his best after a violent death." It sounded derisive. "But I just can't get away from the thought that even in life he was not . . . how shall I put it . . . he could hardly be called . . . Jan-Willem was not a good-looking man, was he?"

She looked him straight in the eyes. Her eyes glowed with a strange light.

"What you're trying to say," she answered sharply, "is that I married Jan-Willem for reasons other than his physical attraction . . . for money."

"Yes," said DeKok, "that's exactly what I mean."

She pressed her lips together. Her hands balled into fists. For several seconds she stared outside. Then she turned back to DeKok.

"I'll be frank with you, Mr. DeKok," she said tonelessly. "I've been bought."

DeKok stared at her.

"Bought?" he repeated slowly.

She nodded savagely.

"A woman doesn't like to admit it and it's often called something else. But I've been bought. You see," she rushed on, "Jan-Willem wasn't married, had never been married and he was close to forty. Apparently he had never met a woman who liked him enough . . . who would have him. When I came to the bank as a young girl, he invited me for a visit to his parents. He was already an Assistant Director and I was flattered. His parents were known to be rich people, very rich people. After dinner they took me aside. Apparently my visit had been well prepared. They were exceedingly well informed. They knew just about everything about me . . . everything . . . about my father . . . how he used to make a living . . . the poverty of my youth. After they had told me everything, they made me an offer." She fell silent, struggled with painful memories. "Marry Jan-Willem . . . in exchange for a life of luxury," she added.

Again she paused, shook her head as if to ban some unpleasant thought. The discreet aroma of an expensive perfume wafted across the table. Vledder and DeKok remained silent as well. After a while she continued.

"Please understand me, I don't want to make it sound worse than it was. I was hardly an innocent little girl. My parents had raised me liberally and living near the Red Light District soon opened my eyes. I was never especially prim and proper and I have had several relationships with men. I wasn't tricked into it, trapped, or anything like that. On the contrary, I knew right from the start exactly what I was doing."

"You accepted their offer," said DeKok.

She stared sadly into the distance and sighed deeply.

"Oh, well," she said. "In the beginning, the first years weren't too bad, I loved the extra freedom that money inevitably

15

provides. I could afford anything I wanted. And Jan-Willem? Well, as you mentioned . . . not exactly an Adonis. But in the beginning he was friendly, attentive and considerate. That's the time our children were born." Again there was a brief pause. She folded her hands on the table in front of her. "Only later did he change markedly. He became moody, stayed away from home longer and longer, became nasty to the kids. And his sexual desires, that had always been a bit strange, became so extreme that in the end I could no longer indulge him." She swallowed. "At such moments he hit me. He was big and strong and he behaved like an animal. I don't want to go into details, but I can show you the scars and bruises on my skin . . . everywhere, except my face." She hid her face in her hands. "He was always careful of my face," she spoke from behind her hands. "And when he was in that mood, I just let him go on, waited until he had cooled off. But it was unbearable. It was unendurable. Finally it became so bad, that he would no longer wait until we were alone. In the presence of strangers . . . even in front of the children . . . he would hit and humiliate me." She uncovered her face. "I should have left, but I stayed because of the children. Of course, I complained to friends, family, acquaintances. In some detail. It was hardly a secret. Everybody knew that I . . . that I . . ."

"... wanted him dead?" suggested DeKok.

She nodded slowly, a distant look in her eyes.

"Sometimes I feel that I am actually the one who killed him."

DeKok studied the tired, resigned, almost apathetic look on her face.

"And did you . . . Josephine?"

Her eyes filled with tears. She rested her head on her arms and cried.

Slowly DeKok stood up. He looked down on her shaking shoulders. His hand hesitantly stroked her blonde hair. He was unsure of himself, confused.

"Or was it your father?"

2

From Hotel-Restaurant *Beehive* the two Inspectors walked back toward Warmoes Street. It had stopped sleeting and the wind was less strong, but it was still raining hard.

DeKok raised the collar of his coat and pulled the brim of his hat deeper into his eyes. The long forgotten toffee appeared in his hand and he slowly removed the wrapper. He put the paper back in his pocket and the toffee in his mouth.

The story of the young woman had touched him. He realized she must have lived in a sort of hell for a long time. He wondered if Jan-Willem's parents were aware of the deviate behavior of their son when they offered him in marriage to Josephine. It was passing strange that the arrangements by the parents had been so solidly prepared.

He could understand how, considering her character, Josephine Haar had accepted the offer. He well remembered that she had once filed a complaint against her father for burglary because she felt that enough was enough. It affected her good name as well, but that had not stopped her. Josephine had always resolutely sought her own way and had never been one to compromise. Perhaps that is why Handy Henkie loved and honored his daughter so. Was there a connection between that and the sudden demise of Henkie's son-in-law? If so, to what extent? Or was Jan-Willem's death not all that sudden. Was it the result of thorough and careful preparation? DeKok's thoughts wandered and returned to the past, to the many confrontations with Josephine's father. In his hey-day Handy Henkie had been an exemplary burglar, a man, who always carefully planned his crimes, who paid attention to the tiniest detail. If Handy Henkie had anything to do with Jan-Willem's killing, the police would have their hands full.

DeKok rubbed the rain from his face. Why had Henkie insisted that he have a talk with Josephine? In order to predispose him, DeKok, kindly toward the girl . . . the woman? Was it a red herring? DeKok cursed under his breath.

"I want nothing to do with it."

Vledder glanced aside.

"Did you say something?"

DeKok nodded.

"I said that I wanted nothing to do with it. It's not our case. It's a case for Deyssel Street. Period. End of story."

Vledder laughed.

"Nevertheless you'll have to make a report about it."

DeKok seemed surprised.

"About what?"

Vledder gestured.

"Your findings in the murder case. The visit from Henkie in the middle of the night and the recent interrogation of Josephine."

DeKok was angry.

"That was no interrogation," he said loudly. "It has nothing to do with me as a cop. It was just an informal discussion . . . between two people who happened to know each other from earlier days."

"Those two are involved with a murder. And you'll have to file a 'contact report' as they call it in the States."

"What sort of nonsense is that?"

"Well, when an agent, or an official of the United States has any contact at all with the opposition, they have to file a contact report. To protect themselves and also in order to let their superiors decide whether or not to follow up on it."

DeKok halted in mid stride and looked at his younger colleague.

"First of all," he said with emphasis, "I have not had any contact with the 'opposition' as you're pleased to call it. Secondly, what earthly good would such a report do? Do you really think Deyssel Street wants it, or needs it? There is nothing concrete, nothing you can put your finger on. All right, Josephine had a bad marriage. But they'll discover that soon enough on their own. They can always interrogate her themselves."

Vledder grinned.

"There's an obvious difference. She will not be as forthcoming with some cops from Deyssel Street as she was with you."

"Josephine trusts me."

"She does?"

"What's that supposed to mean?"

Vledder raised his hands in the air.

"Josephine only told us how unhappily she agreed to get married and what a disaster her marriage turned out to be."

"And?"

Vledder sighed.

"Did you search her room to see if there was a weapon there? A weapon, incidentally, that might be the same make and caliber as that which killed her husband. Did you ask her for an alibi for the night of the murder?" He shook his head. "No, you just listened to her story, like a good father-confessor. She never answered the two specific questions you asked her. Did you, or your father do it?"

DeKok walked on with his head down. Vledder's criticism was justified. But he knew why. There was a certain dualism in his mind. The ethics of his profession battled the admiration he had for Handy Henkie ... a long time ago ... opponent and friend.

* * *

They entered Warmoes Street station and Meindert Post, the Watch Commander, gestured for them from behind his desk.

"DeKok," he roared, even before they had come close enough, "there's a guy upstairs, waiting for you. I told him you weren't in, but he said he'd wait."

DeKok nodded his thanks and climbed the stairs to the next floor. Vledder followed close behind. On the bench outside the detective room they saw a corpulent man in his forties. He was dressed stylishly, in an expensive suit, a Cashmere overcoat and a white silk scarf. An expensive hat was on the bench next to him. DeKok came closer, looked at the strawberry blond hair and recognized "Red" Bakker, a man who, in times gone by, sometimes teamed up with Handy Henkie.

Red Bakker did not have a good reputation in the underworld. He was known as a man who, if necessary, easily betrayed his associates in exchange for either a lighter sentence, or immunity from prosecution.

DeKok motioned for Bakker to follow them into the room. DeKok hung up his wet raincoat and took Bakker to one of the small interrogation rooms. Vledder already had his ubiquitous notebook ready.

The three on them sat around the table in the small room. DeKok looked at Red Bakker for several seconds and managed to produce a winning smile.

"It's starting to look like a reunion," said DeKok. "Last night Handy Henkie and today you."

Red Bakker blinked his eyes rapidly.

"Reunion? Who's talking about reunion. I've done with the past. I'm out of it. It's been at least ten years since my last conviction."

"What do you do for a living, now?"

Red Bakker sighed a pitiful sigh.

"I've been declared 'unfit for the work force' . . . my back. I can't work anymore. Never again. I've a small pension."

DeKok cocked his head.

"I never knew you worked long enough to earn a pension."

Red Bakker looked insulted.

"I was in construction," he said, "I was a brick-layer."

DeKok smiled.

"And you can live on your pension?"

"Ach, what can I say? It's too much to die and not enough to live."

DeKok stretched out a hand to the lapels of the expensive suit and felt the material with the expertise of a tailor. Then he opened the front of the coat and looked at the label. A sarcastic grin played around his mouth.

"Good thing you can buy bargain clothes with your limited income."

Red Bakker was indignant.

"I'm not required to give you an accounting, DeKok." His voice sounded angry and irritated. "I'm here at the request of an old mate. It's just that Henkie asked me, or I would never have come." He paused and rubbed a finger along the inside of his collar. "His daughter is in trouble."

DeKok feigned surprise.

"Really . . . how's that?"

Red looked sad.

"They found her man, somewhere in a park, with three bullets through his chest and the girl was stupid enough to tell everybody who would listen that she wanted to get rid of him."

"And?"

"Well, the crazy thing is, that she didn't want to get rid of him at all."

DeKok's eyebrows suddenly came to life. For a brief moment it seemed as if they danced several millimeters higher than their normal position. They spread, came together and then, just as suddenly came to rest. Almost anyone who had ever seen the phenomenon did not believe their eyes. The usual reaction was a brief, stunned silence and then the observer would shake his, or her head, as if to clear their vision. Almost nobody ever believed they had seen what had so obviously happened.

Vledder was more familiar with the sight than most, but lately he had concentrated on watching the reaction of those who saw it, rather than allow himself to be absorbed by the unusual sight. Vledder looked at Bakker and the result was predictable. It had the added effect of making Red Bakker completely unsure of himself.

"How do you know?" asked DeKok, as if nothing had happened.

Red Bakker licked dry lips. Vledder was familiar with that reaction as well. DeKok's eyebrows took on a life of their own at the most unexpected moments and Vledder had never been able to determine with certainty that DeKok was even aware of it.

"Well, how do you know?" repeated DeKok.

"Well ... see here, DeKok ... let's play open card, all right? I ... I don't come here because I like it, or want to. I ... eh, I don't exactly have happy memories about this place. It took a while before I could be convinced to come here at all, let me tell you." Now that DeKok's eyebrows were again behaving normally, Bakker seemed to regain some confidence. "I don't

24

like to take chances," said the ex-criminal. "I don't mind doing a favor for an old mate, but I don't exactly look forward to being locked up in one of those dungeons you call cells, here in this rat-trap. That's why I first talked to my lawyer to ask if I could tell you the story. You understand? To see if I ran any risk."

"What story?"

"I," said Red Bakker, moving uneasily in his chair, "sometimes still see Henkie. In the streets, in a bar. You know how it is. You talk about this and that, family, whatever. Henkie told me that his daughter has such a miserable life with that guy of hers. Apparently he hit her. Henkie said at one time, just in passing, you understand, that he would like to kick the guy into the next world." He paused, pulled a handkerchief from a pocket and wiped the sweat from his forehead. "I knew that Henkie's daughter had married some rich stinker, a guy that laterally *swam* in money. I also knew that the girl had married under community property laws." He made a vague gesture. "Well, that gave me an idea,"

"What sort of idea?" DeKok's voice was expressionless.

"To make a little extra."

"To profit from some contemplated crime, no doubt."

Bakker shrugged.

"Call it what you want," he said resignedly. "Everybody was born with a number of talents and has to make the best of them. Anyway, one day, when I was sure the guy wouldn't be home, I went to Amstelveen and rang the bell at Josephine's house. She knew me from the old days and invited me in. I asked how things were and said that her father had told me she had such a rough deal." Again he wiped the sweat away. "Then I asked her what it was worth to her."

"What?"

Red Bakker looked uneasy. His nostrils quivered and when he spoke his voice quavered.

"Well, I mean, I know some guys who'd be happy to earn a few grand for a neat job of cleaning up."

"You mean, you have contacts who would be willing to kill someone in exchange for payment. Anybody, as long as the payment is adequate."

"Something like that . . . yes."

DeKok swallowed.

"What was Josephine's reaction?"

Red Bakker spread his arms in a gesture of surrender.

"That's the reason I'm here. She rejected the idea out of hand. Did not even want to think about. She practically chased me off the premises. You see, DeKok, she didn't want that guy dead . . . not at all."

* * *

When Red Bakker had left, Vledder looked at his mentor. The young man was shocked.

"Have we come so far, in Holland, that professional killers are available for hire? We've never, as far as I know, run into that before, here."

DeKok gestured vaguely.

"If you can't find them in Holland, you can always find them abroad. Our borders are always open . . . for everybody." He shrugged his shoulders. "On the other hand, it's entirely possible that Red was just bluffing. If Josephine had been willing to pay ready cash for the murder of her husband . . . he would have had it made."

"I don't understand . . ." said Vledder, confused.

DeKok leaned back in his chair.

"It's really very simple. Once Josephine had paid the money, Red Bakker would have come back, again and again . . . without ever hiring a professional killer. And Josephine would have been powerless to stop it. She would be forced to remain silent. All she could have done was pay . . . and pay . . . and pay."

"But why . . . surely there were no witnesses?"

DeKok grinned.

"Rest assured that Red Bakker would have made sure to have proof of the transaction. So . . . then what? Josephine would never be able to admit publicly that she had paid money to have her husband killed."

"Just dirty blackmail."

"Blackmail is *always* dirty. To my mind the only thing worse is crimes against children. It takes a special kind of person to do either. And I have an idea that Red Bakker has been living quite high on the hog from the proceeds of blackmail . . . for a considerable number of years."

Vledder shook his head with irritation.

"Well, I still don't understand any of it. Why would Bakker have to tell us this, or anything. All it gets him is that we're likely to take a closer look at his current criminal affairs."

DeKok rubbed his chin thoughtfully.

"I think," He said, "that Josephine must have told her father about Red's visit . . . and his offer. And now that Jan-Willem has been killed, Henkie is worried for his daughter. He's afraid that she will be blamed for his death."

Vledder's face cleared up.

"I understand," he exclaimed enthusiastically. "In order to help Josephine in advance, so to speak, he forces Red Bakker to tell us the story about the failed attempt to have Jan-Willem killed on Josephine's orders."

"Very good," nodded DeKok. "Red Bakker's tale is supposed to be the proof that Josephine, despite her remarks, never really wished her husband dead . . . in any case it would prove that she backed down from the consequences of such a plan."

"Shrewd idea of Henkie."

"I had not expected anything else."

Vledder grabbed a chair and straddled it backward, resting his arms on the back of the chair.

"But how," he wanted to know, "could Henkie force Red Bakker to do anything?"

"I think," grinned DeKok, "that Henkie knows more about Red's past, and present, than Bakker would like him to know . . . dark secrets that never came into the full, judicial light of day."

"Blackmail?"

DeKok placed his feet on the table and searched his pockets. He finally found a peppermint and after a casual inspection, put it in his mouth. He sucked contently for several seconds. Then he sighed.

"Blackmail, my boy," he said tiredly. "Believe me, the world is full of blackmail."

Adjutant Kamphouse passed by and tossed a stack of the latest police notices through the open door of the interrogation room on the table in front of DeKok. Vledder took the stack and started reading.

Suddenly his eyes opened wide.

DeKok looked a question.

"Something the matter?"

"They arrested Josephine Haar."

"What!?"

Vledder nodded.

"On suspicion of murdering her husband."

3

They left the interrogation room and returned to their desks. Vledder immediately accessed his computer and started entering all relevant information from Red Bakker's interview, as well as bits and pieces he culled, according to a system of his own, from the various reports. His notebook was on one side and the stack of reports on the other side of his busy fingers.

DeKok looked at the activity of his young colleague, shrugged and went to stand in front of the window behind his own desk. For a while he remained lost in contemplation of the rooftops of his beloved Amsterdam. Suddenly he turned around and leaned his back against the window sill.

"The arrest must have taken place shortly after we left her at the *Beehive* restaurant," said DeKok, easily making his voice carry toward Vledder, despite the constant clamor in the rest of the room. "You said the report was dated at eleven thirty-five. They must have known she was staying at the *Beehive*."

DeKok crunched the last of his peppermint between his strong teeth and shook his head in anger.

"They're crazy," he said. "Josephine didn't do it."

Vledder shook his head.

"You mustn't say that. Our colleagues in Deyssel Street must have enough evidence. After all, it's *their* case."

DeKok growled something unintelligible.

"What?" asked Vledder.

"Before you can make an arrest, you must have *a reasonable suspicion of guilt*. That's the Law."

He pushed himself away from the window sill and went to the coat rack.

"Now what?" asked Vledder. "Where are you going?"

DeKok planted his ridiculous little hat firmly on gray hair.

"I'm going to Deyssel Street . . . I want to ask them how *reasonable* their suspicions are."

* * *

"Extremely reasonable." Inspector Peter Arend Weingarter nodded emphatically. "Absolutely! We have convincing reasons to suspect that Josephine Haar killed her husband."

DeKok gave him a penetrating look.

"Just like that . . . by herself?"

Weingarter hesitated.

"As to that . . . eh, we have no direct evidence. I'll admit that. But she's certainly involved. We assume that she hired someone else to do it."

"A hired killer?"

Inspector Weingarter nodded slowly, avoiding DeKok's gaze. "A hired killer," he said finally, pensively. Then, with more certainty: "Indeed. In any case, someone who has been promised a lot of money for killing her husband."

"Who?"

Weingarter gestured vaguely, rubbed the back of his head and again seemed to lose some of his conviction.

"That . . . eh, . . . we don't know . . . yet. We're hoping, of course, that Josephine will volunteer that information. But she hasn't said a word during her first interrogation."

DeKok was annoyed.

"Where, by all that's sane, have you found this fairy-tale about a hired killer?"

Weingarter gave him a pitying, somewhat arrogant smile.

"That is no fairy-tale. The killer was promised ten thousand ... cash ... as soon as the job had been completed to the satisfaction of the wife." The young Inspector sighed. "Josephine Haar had the money ready ... apparently she had already taken it from the bank. We're still checking that."

DeKok spread his arms in a gesture of despair.

"And how, may I ask, did you gain this knowledge?"

"From the victim's parents."

"The parents of Jan-Willem Hoffman?" asked DeKok, disbelief in his voice.

Inspector Weingarter merely nodded.

When DeKok kept staring at him, Weingarter relented.

"They are extremely reliable people," said the Deyssel Street cop, "take my word for it. I went to inform them of the death of their son and asked, as is customary, if they knew of anything that could help explain his sudden death. Rembrandt Park, where he was found, is known as a meeting place for homosexuals. Perhaps, I thought, Jan-Willem was bi-sexual and used the park for his homosexual encounters. In any case, I felt I should consider it. Of course, I didn't say it that way to the parents, but they seemed to understand me. They told me that they had, over the years, noticed certain sadistic characteristics in their son, much to their regret, but ... and I believe them ... they had never noticed any homosexual tendencies. Then I steered the conversation toward the daughter-in-law and the grandchildren. At that point I had the feeling they were holding something back. The straight answers disappeared, you know what I mean? But I persisted and eventually the father told me that about a month ago they had been visited by a man. To make a long story short, the man had told them that their son's life was in danger. In exchange for some compensation, he would be willing to disclose what sort of danger to expect."

"And he named Josephine Haar?"

"Exactly . . . Jan-Willem's wife."

DeKok chuckled.

"And how did this well-informed person know all that?"

"According to the man, Josephine had contacted him herself and asked him to take care of the problem for her. The man was interested, at first. Ten thousand is not something you turn down every day. But in the end his conscience got the better of him. That's why he did not accept the tempting offer and decided to inform the parents, instead."

DeKok rubbed the bridge of his nose with a little finger. The he lowered the finger and stared at it for several seconds. Finally he pointed the finger at Weingarter.

"Who is that guy?"

Weingarter shrugged his shoulders.

"We don't know that yet. But it will only be a matter of days. Jan-Willem's parents gave us an excellent description . . . about forty, a full, round face, thin, reddish hair."

"Red Bakker."

Weingarter seemed stunned.

"Red Bakker . . . you *know* him?"

DeKok nodded slowly.

"A rat."

* * *

Vledder manoeuvred the old VW through town with casual ease. The communication gear crackled with a report about a collision. With an absent-minded gesture DeKok reached over and shut off the equipment. Then he slid down in his seat and started

32

rummaging in the glove compartment. With a look of triumph on his face he unearthed a candy bar. Thoughtfully he removed the wrapper and took the first satisfying bite.

"Red Bakker has always been a sleazy character," said DeKok with his mouth full. "A first class sneak. Actually, I'm surprised that so far nobody has slipped a piece of steel between his ribs."

Vledder was still angry.

"Where in the world does one get the nerve to tell a story like that to a couple of old people." He shook his head in disbelief. "And they paid him three thousand in gratitude for the information."

DeKok swallowed the last of his candy bar. It had been a small one and with a regretful look on his face he tossed the spent wrapper in the little trash-can Vledder kept in the car, where it joined at least a dozen previously discarded wrappers. Then he answered Vledder:

"Ach, you see, he could do that easily, there was little risk. If Jan-Willem had stayed alive, nobody would have been the wiser. But, of course, Red got into trouble when Josephine's husband was really killed. Suddenly his story became important."

"Is Deyssel Street going to let her go, now?"

"I don't think so," said DeKok. "They probably cannot let her go, even if they check with the Judge-Advocate. First they'll have to find Red Bakker and then they will have to confront him with the parents of Jan-Willem."

"Then what?"

"Then there are two possibilities ... either Red Bakker sticks to his story, but then he's in conflict with the story he told us ... or, he admits that he presented the parents with *a tissue of* *fabrications** in order to induce them to fork over three thousand guilders. In that case he risks prosecution for slander and fraud.

Vledder grinned from ear to ear.

"Either way, uneasy lies the head of Red Bakker."

"You're right and it couldn't happen to a nicer guy. Of course, for Josephine it's important that he's located as soon as possible. And I think it might be a good idea to whisper something into Handy Henkie's ear. He has more ways and means to locate the elusive Mr. Bakker than do we."

Vledder stole a quick glance at his mentor.

"I've always thought it a bit strange that you seem to have such an admiration for Henkie ... after all, he's a common burglar."

DeKok scratched the back of his neck, a sheepish look on his face.

"Well, not a *common* burglar. But one cannot control one's sympathies, or antipathies, especially in this job. We're not machines, after all. People react to one and another. It's inevitable. Handy Henkie was, and is, in my eyes a reasonable person, who, no matter how daft it sounds, practiced his profession of burglar in an *honest* way."

Vledder laughed.

"Then why did he ever team up with Red Bakker. He must have known that guy was no good."

DeKok chewed his lower lip and thought about the answer.

"Well," he said at last, "Handy Henkie did not team up with Red Bakker by preference. He's been disappointed once or twice. But sometimes there was no other way. You see, Red Bakker is related to Henkie's wife ... a cousin, or something."

---

a tissue of fabrications: actual wording describing *lying* in the Dutch Criminal Code.

* * *

For a long time they drove on in silence. Traffic became slower and slower as they approached Warmoes Street. They moved from one gridlocked intersection to the next. DeKok sat up straighter and pushed his hat further back on his head.

"Now you know why I prefer walking," he grumbled. "This city was never built for motorized traffic. It's a mess."

Vledder ignored the remark. He knew that if DeKok had his wish, he would have lived at least a hundred years ago, in the time of horses, buggies and stage coaches.

"Still," said Vledder, "I can't get rid of the feeling that something is wrong. Something does not compute."

"What?"

"About the murder of Jan-Willem Hoffman. Just to be sure, I asked for a copy of the Deyssel Street report on the case."

DeKok reacted predictably.

"I won't read it. We don't need it."

"Then I will read it," said Vledder. "You see, you remarked on it yourself . . . no matter how you look at it, *somebody* put three bullets into Jan-Willem. Somebody who would gain if Jan-Willem were dead."

DeKok nodded.

"All right, I grant you that. But who . . . that's the question." A devilish gleam appeared in the eyes of the older man. "A question for Inspector Peter Arend Weingarter and his eager colleagues in Deyssel Street. We . . . we're *Warmoes* Street . . . and we couldn't care less."

* * *

Handy Henkie looked up at DeKok, who towered over the small ex-burglar by almost a foot.

"One of your colleagues told me you was at Deyssel Street. How was it? Did you talk at Josephine?"

For a moment DeKok paused to consider how much Henkie's speech had improved from his usual gutter language of the past. He still seemed to have some difficulty with the verbs, but his position as a respected instrument-maker and, no doubt, Josephine's influence had increased his vocabulary for the better. It seemed only years ago that Henkie's speech used to resemble that of DeKok's favorite barkeeper, Little Lowee.

DeKok shook his head.

"I told you, Henkie, it isn't my case."

"I'm telling you: she's innocent."

"I can't comment on that."

"Didn't you talk at Red Bakker?"

DeKok nodded.

"Yes, he was here."

"Well . . .?"

The gray sleuth evaded Henkie's eyes. He rubbed the back of his neck with a tired gesture.

"I'm sorry. I could not nullify her arrest on the say-so of Red Bakker."

Henkie raised his arms in a gesture of hopelessness.

"What have they got against her?" he asked despairingly. "They didn't want to tell me. They got any proof?"

DeKok looked at the distraught father.

"Red Bakker *also* told a story to the parents of the deceased and Deyssel Street took *that* story rather seriously."

For a moment Henkie seemed dazed. He looked past DeKok into the distance.

"I can just imagine," he said after a long pause, "What he told those parents. I *knows* how he works. I knows all his dirty tricks." He shook his head dejectedly. "But that he would use them on his own flesh and blood, that . . ." He did not complete the sentence. "How much did they give him?"

"Three thousand. Now, of course, Deyssel Street needs Red Bakker real bad. They want to hear from him *personally* how all this connects. They want to know if he'll stick to his story and that is, needless to say, very important for Josephine." He smiled at the ex-burglar. "As soon as you find Red, why don't you take him to the station yourself . . . alive, you understand? If you mess him up too much, he won't be able to tell them he could have made a mistake."

* * *

After Handy Henkie had left, DeKok seated himself behind his desk. With indolent movements he opened a drawer and took out some files. Some had been in his desk drawer for some time and concerned less urgent cases that nevertheless had to be processed. He stared at them for a while and then opened the center drawer of his desk. Among the usual paper-clips, rubber bands, post-it notes and half-empty pens, he found a roll of licorice drops. With one hand he flipped one of the drops from the roll and with the other he opened the first file.

He read through the reports and evidence files and saw no reason to change his opinion on any of them. He marked them with a dull pencil and put them on the side of his desk, next to the unused terminal of his computer. The computer had been sitting there, unused, since the day it was installed. DeKok was the last cop in Holland that still wrote all his reports, if he wrote reports, in long hand. He had never used a typewriter and saw no need to learn about computers.

Fortunately for him, as well as the Dutch Judicial System, Vledder was a genius on the computer and liked nothing better than to invent new ways of storing, correlating and retrieving odd bits of information. Vledder also had devised a system whereby he could produce almost any kind of report in a minimum amount of time, using the large police data base, his own data base and other bits and pieces of information he had scattered in his various computer files.

DeKok always enjoyed watching Vledder as his fingers moved across the keys at a speed of ninety words a minute, doing incomprehensible things with micros, macros and formats. As he worked, Vledder was heard to mumble to himself, or perhaps he talked to the computer, mused DeKok.

Whatever Vledder's virtuosity, DeKok had never found it necessary to emulate his younger partner.

After finishing his notes, he tossed the files to Vledder, who deftly caught them in one hand. His other hand already clearing his screen of whatever was on it, in order to "polish" DeKok's final reports. The young man smiled happily as he went to work.

DeKok retrieved the roll of licorice drops and had another one.

While Vledder was happily typing away, DeKok put his feet on the desk and looked across the busy detective room without consciously seeing any of it. His thoughts roamed along a magic square shaped by Red Bakker, Handy Henkie, daughter Josephine and Jan-Willem Hoffman. The idea that he had nothing to do with the case, seemed less defensible as he thought about it. On the contrary, he had the oppressive feeling that dark clouds where gathering somewhere, that he was already deeper into the case than he suspected, that he would be forced to participate.

He sighed with exhaustion. Sometimes police work made him weary. Sometimes he felt he saw nothing but the pale, revolting underbelly of society and sometimes it seemed too much.

The phone on his desk rang suddenly. Before he could react, Vledder had already reached over and lifted the receiver. He handed it to DeKok. DeKok had been known to let a phone ring until it stopped by itself. Telephones were another modern invention of which he did not approve.

"DeKok," he said in the mouthpiece.

The Watch Commander was on the other side of the line. DeKok listened and immediately returned to the present. After less than a minute he replaced the receiver gently and looked at Vledder.

"Leave that mess," he said, "and let's go."

"Go where?" asked Vledder as his fingers flew over the keyboard, shutting down his terminal.

"To the building lot for the Metro."

"Building lot?" asked Vledder, getting to his feet.

"Yes, the land near Lastage Road, where they tore down those houses to make room for the new Metro line."

"Why? What's there?"

"A corpse."

"Accident? Heroin?"

"No, murder."

4

Amsterdam's Lastage Road: In the not too distant past the scene of pitched battles between hordes of demonstrators against the razing of old buildings and houses and, the usually young, members of the police force, called into action by a slow and hesitating city government. That day it was a sad, deserted expanse of mud, bordered by dilapidated, abandoned buildings, waiting for the wrecker's hammer. A tall construction mast threw a dim, yellow light across the heaps of rubble. Twisted steel beams and rusty skeletons of reinforced concrete formed bizarre shadows, as in some macabre surrealistic painting. On his back in a stinking mud puddle they found the man. The fingers of a cramped left hand pointed at a broken sewer cover.

DeKok pulled up the slips of his raincoat and squatted down next to the corpse. The man was dead. There was no doubt about that. The mouth hung open and there was a soulless look in the half-closed eyes. On the white shirt, on the left side of the chest were three dark-red spots, close together, almost touching each other.

Vledder leaned forward.

"He didn't have much of a chance," he observed. There was an undertone of pity and revulsion in his voice. "All three of the shots were fatal, right through the heart . . . possibly fired in rapid succession."

DeKok nodded agreement.

"You're right. The murderer was an excellent shot." He looked intently at the face of the man, the high cheekbones, the black hair and the little bit of gray at the temples. "How old do you think?"

Vledder shrugged.

"Hard to say . . . probably late forties. Perhaps a little younger. Typical businessman."

DeKok seemed not to have heard the answer to his question. Slowly he rose from his squatting position and looked around. To the right, on a yellow wall he saw the word "Forge" in square, blue letters. That was the place where the demonstrators used to gather and where they had issued their "manifestoes" to the city government, demanding that the building of the Metro be halted. A little further away were the waters of the Old Waal and the Crooked Waal, all that remained of the mighty river that split off the Rhine as it entered the Netherlands. They were only four canals away from Warmoes Street and the raucous but cozy Red Light District. But it seemed another world. Both sides of the Crooked Waal and the Old Waal were occupied by houseboats that were moored stem to stern and, in a few cases, side by side. The houseboats were occupied by a varied population, ranging from respectable citizens to crooks and the last of the hippies from the sixties and even a few floating brothels. Within a stone's throw was the famed Inner Bantam Street with its three- and four star restaurants, almost door to door, where impassive Chinese spoiled jaded Amsterdammers and tourists with oriental delicacies.

The gray sleuth scratched the back of his neck. He wondered if there had been anybody, besides the killer, who had heard the shots, or seen the killing, It did not seem likely.

A young constable approached, notebook in hand. He pointed behind him.

"That's the man who found him. I have his name, address and so on, but perhaps you want to talk to him yourself."

DeKok pulled back the sleeve of his coat and looked at his watch.

"Who would be roaming around here at this ungodly hour. Is he a junkie?"

The constable shook his head.

"Just a citizen. He lives close by in one of the houseboats on the Crooked Waal, near Montel Street. He was just walking his dog before going to bed. The animal started to sniff around. When the man went looking for his dog, he found the corpse and called the police."

DeKok pursed his lips.

"That," he admitted, "sounds plausible enough." Then he added: "Just take his statement, complete with time of discovery." He looked at the constable. "What kind of dog?"

The constable grinned.

"A Heinz."

"Heinz? Never heard of that breed."

"Heinz, you know, the ketchup people: 57 varieties. That's the dog . . . a mongrel, at least 57 varieties of dog."

DeKok smiled.

"All right. I'll see your report on my desk tomorrow."

The constable walked away and DeKok turned toward Vledder, who was still looking over the scene of the crime.

"Any shells?"

"I found two, so far." Vledder pointed towards two little sticks pushed into the mud. DeKok leaned forward.

"Looks like 9 mm. All things being equal, there should be three of them."

Bram Weelen, the police photographer, followed by the rest of the forensic team, approached, carefully avoiding the large puddles. He carried a heavy aluminum case hanging by a strap from his shoulder. He waved casually at Vledder and DeKok and glanced at the corpse.

"I'll be damned," he said. "It looks like that guy in Rembrandt Park."

"Never swear *toward* yourself," admonished DeKok, "you might get your wish." Then he looked closely at the photographer. "You were there, were you . . . in Rembrandt park?"

"Yes," said Weelen, "the dead guy on the gravel path there . . . he was in just about the same position. On his back and three shots close together in the region of the heart. If I were you I'd talk to the boys at Deyssel Street."

"We already did," grinned DeKok. "Even *before* we discovered this one."

Bram Weelen found a relatively dry spot and opened his suitcase. Quickly and carefully he assembled his precious Hasselblad.

"They already arrested someone for the Rembrandt Park murder," he said casually, as he lined up for the first set of exposures. "Apparently they have some evidence against the wife of the victim."

DeKok nodded seriously.

"I presume she's still in jail?"

Weelen flashed his first shot. Suddenly, he lowered the camera and looked at the old Inspector.

"But," he said, "then she can never have killed this one." It sounded like a sudden discovery.

"No," answered DeKok. "It's hard to get a better alibi."

Vledder interrupted. He pointed at the corpse.

"Do you think," he asked the photographer, "that this guy and the one in Rembrandt Park were hit by the same killer?"

Weelen made a defensive gesture.

"Hey, hey, hey!" he protested. "I'm just the photographer. I just take the pictures. Your job is to solve the crimes. All I'm saying that the wounds seem identical. I noticed that right off." He paused. "Any shells?"

"I found two so far," said Vledder. He pointed at the forensic team which had started to rope off the area. "They'll probably find the third one."

"So, a pistol."

"Obviously. A revolver doesn't throw out spent shells, unless you take them out yourself."

Weelen gestured with his camera.

"Well, if the guys from the lab confirm that these shells and the shells from Rembrandt Park are fired from the same weapon, you're quite a bit ahead."

"How's that . . . ahead of what?"

"In finding the perpetrator of the two killings."

DeKok shook his decisively.

"Even if the bullets and the entries are identical . . . it doesn't have to be the same perp. The weapon could have been handled by more than one person." He turned toward Vledder, pulling him away from the busy experts who were now swarming all over the place. "Let's assume that Josephine is indeed the killer of Jan-Willem . . . after she's done the deed, she makes sure her father gets the pistol. Handy Henkie now uses the same weapon to commit a second murder . . . just to prove that his daughter is innocent. Henkie is capable of doing such a thing . . . for Josephine."

Doctor Koning, the old Coroner, tapped DeKok on the shoulder.

"Do you mind?" he said in a peeved voice.

DeKok hastily got out of the way and greeted the old man heartily.

"I apologize, Doctor, I didn't see you arrive." He looked over the old man's shoulder and saw an ambulance parked near Knight Street. "You came with the Medical Service?"

The old Coroner, as usual, was dressed in formal, striped pants, shoes with spats and a cut-away coat. On his head was a large, greenish Garibaldi hat. Instead of a raincoat, he wore a large cape that would have looked good on a Musketeer. But the old man did not look ridiculous. Somehow it suited him. DeKok merely saw him as an old friend from an earlier age and he approved highly of the old man.

"Yes," answered the doctor. "My own driver is sick. Young people don't have any stamina, anymore. The Morgue vehicle is on another call and that was the nearest transportation." He pointed at the corpse. "Is that the patient?"

"Patient," chuckled DeKok. "Corpse is more like it. I don't think there's much to be done."

"Really, DeKok, I used the term 'patient' only metaphorically, you know. No need to make jokes about it."

"I beg your pardon, doctor, you're absolutely right. No joke was intended."

The old man gave DeKok a stern look and then knelt down next to the corpse. His knees creaked audibly. He felt both cheeks and the forehead. Then he pulled back the eyelids and looked at the eyes. With a reverent gesture he closed the lifeless eyes after his examination.

"The man is dead," he said formally.

"Thank you, doctor," replied DeKok, just as formally. According to Dutch law only now had the man officially become a corpse.

"Not long ago," volunteered the Coroner.

DeKok looked surprised. The old man was usually very reticent about volunteering information at the site of the crime.

"How long ago," asked DeKok eagerly.

The eccentric Coroner answered hesitantly.

"I . . . I've probably already said too much. You see, I shouldn't have said a thing. You understand, DeKok, these things should really be determined by the official autopsy."

"Yes, of course, doctor, but perhaps you can give us a hint?"

"Very well, then, but you must consider this a very preliminary conclusion. He died perhaps an hour or two ago. The body is still a bit warm and in this place, at this time, considering the corpse is in a puddle, there must be a strong cooling down process."

DeKok nodded.

"Can you perhaps be a little more exact, doctor?"

The Coroner sighed.

"Well, I've brought it on myself, I suppose. I started it, so to speak." He looked at his old-fashioned watch which he dug up from a vest pocket. "You can presume, I think, that he was still alive around ten o'clock. That's all I can say." He turned around. "Really, DeKok, I've already said more than I should have," he added as he stepped away. A constable hastened near in order to escort the old man toward the waiting ambulance.

Bram Weelen approached DeKok.

"That's it for me, then, unless you need something else."

DeKok shook his head and Weelen packed his equipment back into his suitcase. As he prepared to leave, one of the forensic team handed him a plastic bag with three shells.

Weelen accepted the bag and nodded. With his free hand he waved good bye.

"I'll drop off the shells at the lab, on my way," Weelen assured DeKok. "Tomorrow morning, first thing, you'll have your pictures," he added.

DeKok waved back.

"Don't make it too late and say hello for me to your wife."

Two paramedics approached with a stretcher. DeKok nodded for them to proceed. He watched as they lifted the corpse on the stretcher, covered it with a tarpaulin and carried it off. No body bag this time, he thought. He idly wondered why ambulances did not carry body bags but then forgot the question as Vledder walked up.

"Just follow the ambulance," he told his partner. "Before they stick him in the drawer, be sure to collect everything from his pockets."

"All right," said Vledder.

"We still don't know who he is," added DeKok thoughtfully. He rubbed his chin. "Maybe he has a wife and children somewhere, waiting for him."

"Then what?" asked Vledder.

"What do you mean?"

"After I've emptied his pockets and stuff?"

"Get back to the station, I'll be waiting for you. If there is a wife and children, we'll have to notify them, tonight, or as early as possible in the morning."

Vledder nodded and walked toward the VW. DeKok looked after him until he saw the red tail-lights disappear into the evening fog. For several more minutes he remained, deep in thought. Then, without another glance at the scene, he walked away through the mud until he reached a paved piece of road.

Murder, he thought, it's a sad business.

* * *

Vledder read out loud, one eye on his computer terminal and another on his voluminous notes.

"Alexander Peetersen, with double 'e', forty-two years of age, accountant by profession, address: 372 Queen Emma Lane in Amsterdam." He folded closed the driver's license and changed his tone of voice. "That's him for sure. The same name appears in the Dutch Passport. He looks a few years younger in the Passport, but the likeness is unmistakable."

He walked over to the table they had pushed between their desks and on which all the possessions of the deceased had been displayed. He replaced the driver's license.

DeKok was tired and longed for his bed.

"Any stamps in the Passport?"

Vledder lifted the document from the table and rifled through the pages.

"A few border crossings. Stamps from Airport Customs at Schiphol and some British stamps. But you know how it is nowadays. They hardly ever look at your passport anymore, what with the EEC and all."

"Any money?"

"More than five hundred guilders in a wallet and some small change in his pockets."

"Well," sighed DeKok, "that probably eliminates robbery."

"I think so," agreed Vledder. "It doesn't look at all like robbery. As far as I can tell, nothing has been taken. He also had a heavy, gold cigarette case and a gold cigarette lighter. There was a platinum ring with an impressive diamond on his little finger. I think," he added, "that the late Mr. Peetersen must have lost some weight since he first got the ring. It posed no trouble at all, it came off quite easily." He paused. "If he had been attacked by junkies . . ." He did not complete the sentence. "Anyway," he concluded, "we were lucky to find him so quickly."

"Yes," agreed DeKok. "It would have been a lot more difficult. Any other possessions?"

"Nothing of real value, except a set of credit cards, including American Express and Diner's Club."

"A man of the world."

"With an income about which the average person can only dream."

"The average person is still alive," chided DeKok gently. "Did he have a pocket agenda, or a notebook on him?"

"Oh, yes, an expensive one, naturally. Leather with gold initials. But it's practically empty. Not a single note or reminder. Just a lot of phone numbers."

"Married?"

"Hard to say." shrugged Vledder. "No photos. No photos of children, either. We'll have to wait until the morning and check with Town Hall. Unless you want to drive to Queen Emma Lane now, to see if there's a wife."

DeKok shook his head.

"No, it will have to wait. It's a beastly hour anyway. If there is a wife, it will be better to face her in the morning." He waddled over to the table and let his eyes roam over the displayed items. "Did he have that with him as well?" he asked, pointing at a street map of Amsterdam.

"Yes, folded in an outside pocket of his jacket. It got a little wet from the puddle where we found him."

DeKok pulled on his lower lip and let it plop back with an irritating sound. He repeated the annoying gesture several times.

"Peetersen was a native Amsterdammer, wasn't he?"

"Well, he was born in Amsterdam, according to his papers."

DeKok picked up the map.

"Why would a native Amsterdammer carry a street map of this city?" He unfolded the map and spread it on the table. Suddenly he leaned closer. "Look," he said hoarsely, "a mark."

Vledder came to look as well.

"The place where he was killed!"

5

Adjutant Kamphouse tossed a heavy, brown envelope on Vledder's desk.

"Delivered this morning from Deyssel Street," he clarified. "Complete copies of all reports concerning the Rembrandt Park murder."

Vledder opened the envelope and glanced through the contents. Then he put it all in a drawer of his desk.

"The murder of Jan-Willem Hoffman," Vledder explained to Kamphouse.

"Is that your case? I thought I saw a notation in the night log that you have another murder on your hands."

"Yes, that's right. Last night, around midnight, near the construction site for the new Metro line. One Alexander Peetersen . . . three bullets through the heart."

"Any connection with that . . . eh, that Hoffman?"

Vledder became pompous.

"There are, we think, certain points of congruence. I will review the Deyssel Street reports as soon as I have a moment. I've no time now. I've a date with the pathologist."

Adjutant Kamphouse walked away, distributing larger and smaller packets of information to the various desks. DeKok, who had ignored Kamphouse and his conversation with Vledder, now looked up from his careful unwrapping of a stick of chewing gum.

"What time is the autopsy?"

"Ten fifteen. Dr. Rusteloos asked me to be on time."

"Ask him to look for rice."

"Rice?" repeated Vledder.

"In the stomach of the victim," explained DeKok patiently. "It's not at all outside the realm of possibilities that Peetersen had a meal in Bantam Street before he was killed. According to Dr. Koning he was still alive at ten o'clock. So, he could have dined between six and eight. The food in the stomach has not yet been digested and, ergo, recognizable."

"Aha," exclaimed Vledder. "And if there is rice in the stomach, we can take his picture to the various Chinese and Indonesian restaurants and ask if he was seen with anybody."

DeKok pointed a finger at Vledder.

"Very good," he said, stowing the chewing gum behind his teeth. "Of course, he could have eaten Italian, or whatever. But that's of less importance at the moment. Just ask the good doctor what I'm after and he'll do the rest. It isn't the first time he has done an autopsy." He smiled. "I asked him once, years ago, how many autopsies he had performed in his life and he told me that if they had all been alive, it would fill a small town."

Vledder grinned.

"By now it has probably become a large town. Anything else you want?"

"Check the clothes. they're still there. Look for bullets in the clothes. Sometimes a bullet will penetrate the body, but get stuck in the clothing of the victim."

"Anything else?"

DeKok shook his head.

"No, thanks, just say hello for me. When you're finished come back here."

"*Oui, mon colonel*," joked Vledder and went to get his coat. As he put on his coat, he looked back at DeKok. "And you, what will you be doing?"

DeKok also stood up from behind his desk and grabbed his raincoat and his little hat.

"I'm going to pay a visit."

"The sorrowing widow?"

Half in and half out of his coat, DeKok halted. Briefly his eyebrows flared.

"Perhaps," he said slowly, "perhaps the widow is not sorrowing at all."

* * *

DeKok proceeded at a snail's pace from Amsterdam, along the towing path toward Purmerend. On his left, heavily laden barges moved toward the city on the North-Holland Canal, which connects the northern tip of the province of Holland with Amsterdam and the industrial areas around Zaandam, where most of Holland's chocolate is made and Alkmaar, "cheese capital" of Holland.

DeKok was so absorbed by the barges that he almost ran a red light where he was supposed to turn off. He stopped in the middle of the intersection. An angry driver pointed his finger at his forehead. DeKok made a gesture indicating that he fully agreed with the opinion of the other driver. Then he moved the gearshift in the wrong slot three times in a row and released a deep sigh when he finally managed to drive off in the desired direction without being hit by other traffic.

DeKok did not like cars and he had no feeling at all for engines. He usually tried to take off in third gear and always had to consult the schematic on top of the gearshift, before being able to move in reverse. DeKok was a danger on the road and nobody knew that better than himself. He knew he was the worst driver in Holland, probably all of Europe, maybe the world. The distance to Purmerend was too far to do conveniently on a bicycle and he had already several times regretted his decision not to take the train. He stopped at the side of the road and consulted the piece of paper on which he had written the address.

"Heron's Park," he murmured to himself. "Number 218." It was a new neighborhood of single family residences, near Purmerend, part of expansion plan "Overwhere II."

After some trials and errors he located the entrance to the development and stopped in front of a large rambler-type house, accentuated with decorative white tiles. He locked the car and proceeded over the fine gravel toward the front door. An exceedingly elegant marble nameplate next to the front door announced: *Alexander Peetersen, CPA.*

DeKok rang the bell and listened to the musical sound from inside the house. After about a minute the door was opened by a handsome woman. DeKok estimated her to be in her late thirties. She was tastefully and simply dressed in a brown skirt and a beige blouse with a high collar.

The sleuth lifted his hat and bowed with old-world charm.

"My name is DeKok," he said in a friendly voice. "DeKok with . . . eh, with kay-oh-kay. I'm a police Inspector attached to Warmoes Street Station in Amsterdam."

She looked at him with amazement and DeKok had the opportunity to observe that she had almond-shaped eyes that gave her oval face a special, almost exotic look.

"Police . . . Warmoes Street . . . that's the Red Light District."

Her voice was warm, melodious and with just a hint of fear. DeKok nodded.

"Please don't worry," he said soothingly. "The reputation of Warmoes Street is worse than the reality." He smiled. Then his face sobered and he changed the tone of his voice. "I . . . eh, I came to talk about your husband."

"My husband?"

There was more than just the question in her voice, there was a definite hesitation.

"Yes. Aren't you . . . Mrs. Peetersen?"

She stood up straight, as with new resolve. A slight blush enhanced the attractiveness of her face.

"Indeed," she answered. "I'm Mrs. Peetersen . . . still."

DeKok could taste the tone.

"Your husband has an address in Queen Emma Lane in Amsterdam. According to the City Registry he lived here until about a year ago. He's listed as being married to Margaritha Myerink."

"That's me."

"You do not live together?"

She shook her head and examined the man in front of her. For another moment she hesitated. Then she opened wider the door.

"Won't you come in, Inspector? Would you like some coffee? It's just ready." She closed the front door behind them and led the way to a large L-shaped room with an imposing open hearth. She pointed at deep, comfortable chairs. "Please sit down. Cream and sugar?"

DeKok followed her with his eyes as she walked across shining flagstones toward a large farm-kitchen. During his long career he had learned not to be surprised at anything. But to give up such a house and such a woman . . .

She interrupted his musings.

"Is something the matter with Alex?"

DeKok did not answer.

She placed the steaming coffee on a small table next to his chair and sat down across from him, crossing her legs gracefully.

She looked at him and again DeKok experienced the enchantment of her eyes. It gave him a warm feeling.

"Alex," she said, "has the unfortunate ability to continually get into trouble. Which is the reason we're separated. I had enough."

"Women?"

"That too," she gave him a sad smile. "Perhaps that hurts the most, as a woman. But there were other things."

"Such as?"

"Debts. Alex never knew how to handle money." She gestured around. "If my family had not insisted on a pre-nuptial agreement, this, too, would have been long gone."

"And what about his accounting firm?"

"A few old faithful from the time his father led the concern. In fact, they practically run the business. And a good thing, too." She paused and gave DeKok a penetrating look. "What has Alex done this time?"

DeKok slowly lifted his cup from the little table, stirred and took a sip.

"I ... eh, I don't know what Alex has *done*," he said carefully. "I only know what has happened to him."

There was a wary look in her eyes.

"Has happened?"

DeKok replaced the cup on the saucer. His movements were slow, careful, designed for effect.

"We found your husband late last night. Around midnight. We could not reach you last night." There was regret in his voice. "We did not know your address."

She rose from her chair. She looked down at him.

"Why should you have wanted to reach me?"

DeKok rubbed the back of his neck. He felt helpless, inadequate. He always envied priests and ministers at times like these. In this sort of situation he never seemed to have the right words, the correct sentiments.

"We wanted . . . needed to let you know," he stumbled over the words, "that . . . that your husband . . ."

She stared at him. She suddenly guessed what had happened.

"Is Alex . . . is he dead?"

DeKok nodded, avoiding her eyes.

"Murdered," he said softly.

She nodded slowly in return, almost in rhythm with his movements. Carefully, cautiously she let the words penetrate.

"Murdered," she repeated, "murdered. She sank back into her chair. She folded her hands in her lap. "Murdered . . . how senseless."

DeKok stole a glance at her. The oval face was tight, pale and tense. But there were no tears. The brown eyes looked at him clear and bright.

"Why?"

DeKok chewed his lower lip with indecision.

"We don't know," he said finally. "If we knew the reason, we would be farther along. It is my job to investigate the murder of your husband. Motives are important, vital." He pointed in her direction. "Did your husband have enemies?"

Mrs. Peetersen shrugged her shoulders dispiritedly.

"Alex was very secretive," she said softly. "he never talked to me about his troubles. I've blamed him often enough for that. Alex always felt he shouldn't burden me with his problems. I never knew how he got so far in debt. He would talk about 'mismanagement' . . . but I always felt that he kept the real reason hidden from me."

"Do you have children?"

She sighed.

"A son, Richard. He's seven years old ... was seven in September. He's staying with my mother."

DeKok was embarrassed.

"Did your husband ever hit you, beat you up?"

She frowned.

"Beat me?"

DeKok's face was serious.

"I realize it's an unpleasant subject for you, but did your husband ever use physical force on you. Perhaps in a sudden outburst of anger ... erotic sadism?"

Mrs. Peetersen seemed to withdraw within herself.

"Alex never beat me," she said haughtily, a sharp look in her eyes. "I would not have permitted it." Then her expression softened. "I don't believe that Alex was capable of violence ... any violence. He was faithless, untrustworthy. His difficulties stemmed from a lack of attentiveness. He was careless, you see, like a big spoiled child."

"And you were attracted to that?"

Mrs. Peetersen did not answer directly. Her mouth hardened.

"Regardless, I will make sure that my son, Richard, will know his responsibilities as a man."

"And Alex did not know them?"

"Not always ... usually not."

DeKok rubbed the bridge of his nose with a little finger. The unbending, cool attitude of the woman was not to his liking. It was as if she had built a wall around herself, an impregnable bastion, behind which she carefully protected her innermost feelings.

"Those debts," he asked carefully, "could those have been gambling debts?"

"You want to know if he visited casinos?"

DeKok smiled.

"More money changes hands in illegal gambling establishments than in legitimate casinos. The secret gambling places are very much in vogue. They give credit . . . and there are few limits."

She looked at him searchingly.

"You mean that Alex may have been playing on credit . . . and above his limits?"

"For instance."

Mrs. Peetersen shook her head emphatically.

"I'm more inclined to suspect blackmail."

DeKok had not expected that.

"Blackmail?" he asked. "Do you have any reason to justify that suspicion . . . do you have any proof?"

"No, not exactly . . . not at all. It's just a feeling."

DeKok stood up. The conversation was not going as he had expected, or wanted. It seemed better to bring the interview to an end.

"What sort of car did your husband drive?"

She shrugged her shoulders.

"An American car, of course. I think the last one was a Chevrolet, or was it General Motors? I don't know exactly. He probably has a new one already."

DeKok moved in the direction of the hall.

"Who would know? Except for his driver's license, we found no other automobile documentation."

Mrs. Peetersen followed him.

"Perhaps they'll know at the office." Suddenly her voice changed. "And *she* will know."

DeKok turned suddenly. The changed tone had surprised him.

"Who?"

For the first time her tone betrayed an honest emotion.

"Josephine Hoffman."

DeKok swallowed.

"Josephine . . . from Amstelveen?"

Her mouth formed a tight line. Her nostrils quivered and there was hate in her eyes.

"Yes, that . . . that slut from the street . . . for more than a year she's been having an affair with *my* husband."

6

"An affair?"

DeKok nodded.

"For more than a year, according to Mrs. Peetersen."

Vledder grimaced.

"That doesn't look good for Josephine, does it? I have an idea that the Judge-Advocate will be even more reluctant to set her free."

"I don't know," shrugged DeKok. "It doesn't make much sense to first kill your husband and then your lover." He smiled. "A young woman becomes so . . . so neglected that way."

Vledder nodded seriously. He had not understood the joke.

"But no matter which way you look at it . . . both men are from her immediate environment. Somehow the motive must be connected to her as well."

"Aha, so you see Josephine Hoffman as the key to the solution . . . she should be able to give us the vital clue?"

"Yes, either she, or her father, perhaps in combination with Red Bakker."

DeKok leaned his chair back and placed his feet on the desk.

"And how would you apply the motive?"

"Well," gestured Vledder, "we can safely assume that Red Bakker is involved in unsavory businesses . . . blackmail, fraud."

"Granted, but I don't think he's a murderer. Too cowardly."

"He could have someone else *do* it."

"And then what does he get out of it? Red Bakker is a shrewd, sharp guy. A person who is always on the look-out for number one, himself. He's also a man who will avoid the slightest risk." DeKok sighed deeply. "If he's part of the combination you mentioned, that leaves only Handy Henkie as a possible perpetrator. *He* could have motives other than gain. He could have done it to help his daughter. The bond between him and his daughter is very tight." He looked at Vledder. "As I left Purmerend, I even considered Mrs. Peetersen. She's cool one, driven by passion and hatred."

"Hatred? Against whom"

"Against Josephine . . . that slut from the street."

* * *

Vledder was behind the wheel again and at a sedate pace they drove behind the Royal Palace, across Town House Street toward Rose Canal. Vledder looked at DeKok who was chewing on a candy cane.

"You think they'll let us in on it?"

"Sure," grinned DeKok. "Weingarter wouldn't dare refuse. Because of the statement by Mrs. Peetersen, Josephine has also become a part of *our* investigation. We'll have to coordinate things, I'm afraid. By the way, any results from the lab?"

"No, I rang. The investigation is not yet complete, but they promised a report, soon. They were willing to admit that the shells found near Hoffman, were fired from the same weapon that was used on Peetersen."

"And the autopsy?"

"Pretty quick. It took less than an hour and a half. It seems that the older Dr. Rusteloos gets, the faster he works."

"Yes, yes, well?"

"Any of the shots would have been fatal. All three in the heart. According to his calculation, based on the path of the bullets and assuming that Peetersen was standing ... which seems likely ... Dr. Rusteloos concluded that the shooter was a relatively small man, or woman. Unless they shot from the hip. In that case our perpetrator must have been an exceptionally good shot."

"And what about the trajectories in Hoffman's case?"

"Almost identical. I asked especially. Luckily Dr. Rusteloos handled both corpses and he was willing to confirm that both had been killed by the same person."

They drove on in silence. When they stopped in front of the Deyssel Street station-house, DeKok hoisted himself out of the car. Across the roof of the VW he asked:

"Rice?"

Vledder chuckled.

"Oh, yes ... rice. That was a good idea. Shortly before he died, Peetersen ate an elaborate Chinese dinner."

"What have you done about it?"

"I called Fred Prins at once, from the lab. Dr. Rusteloos was still stitching everything back together. Anyway, I asked Fred to take a photo of Peetersen and check out the nearby restaurants. He was already on his way before you returned from Purmerend." He winked. "You took a while, you know. What was the matter? Couldn't find fourth gear?"

DeKok snorted and walked into the station.

* * *

Inspector Weingarter shook hands with DeKok.

"The master sleuth," he said, mildly mocking, "arrives for the second time in our humble abode, this unworthy police station at Deyssel Street. This should be recorded for all posterity. I, personally, shall make an entry in the log ... one-oh-five pee-em ... DeKok was here. I wonder," he added, "if we should not inform the media ..."

Vledder was amused.

"Now you have an idea what I have to put up with," said the young man, "always, by night and by day, to have to work in the spotlight of such a celebrity."

DeKok remained silent and looked from one to the other. Only a slight twinkling in his eyes betrayed that he did not mind having his leg pulled. After a while he turned toward Weingarter.

"How much longer," he asked, "do you intend to keep Josephine *robbed of her freedom?*"*

"There's no question of that," protested Weingarter. "Josephine is a suspect in a murder case. We have reasonable grounds, as I told you before. The Judge-Advocate happens to agree. He's aware of the situation."

DeKok raised his hands in a gesture of surrender.

"All right, all right. Have you found Red Bakker?"

"No," confessed Weingarter. "Red Bakker seems to have gone up in smoke. Disappeared without a trace. Your friend, Handy Henkie, is here at almost every hour of the night and day to ask if we've heard anything about Bakker yet."

DeKok looked pensive.

"He couldn't find him, himself?"

"No, and I'm sure that Henkie has just about mobilized the entire Amsterdam underworld."

---

*robbed of freedom, specific language in Dutch Law.

"But, surely, there have been new developments since my last visit?"

"Sure," nodded Weingarter calmly. "We can add another motive to the existing charges against her."

"Oh, yes? What sort of motive?"

"Josephine had a lover . . . probably for some time. You see, that's another reason she might have wanted her husband dead."

DeKok smiled thinly.

"And who is this mysterious lover?"

Weingarter moved his feet uneasily.

"Well, you see, we don't know yet. But," he continued hastily, "apparently Jan-Willem Hoffman discovered something about an affair his wife was supposed to have with another man. He definitely talked about it with his parents."

"How long ago was that?"

"Less than a month before his death."

"And you don't know the identity of the lover?"

Weingarter shook his head.

"Of course, I discussed it with Josephine, but she refuses to say anything about it. Actually swears she doesn't have a lover."

"Any idea where to look for this lover, who Josephine says doesn't exist?"

"Not a clue."

DeKok grinned broadly. There was just a hint of satisfaction in his eyes.

"We," he said, emphasizing the word, "*we* know." There was a relaxed smile on his face as he pointed over his shoulder. "You'll find him, carefully examined and reassembled in the police lab at Portage Street. He's on ice."

Weingarter's mouth fell open.

"What!?"

DeKok nodded benignly.

"Alexander Peetersen," he said.

* * *

She did not look good. Unkempt. The stay in the police cell at Deyssel Street had affected her beauty. The long blonde hair had been gathered in a pony tail. Her skin was gray, without life, or luster. But her eyes sparkled and darted left and right and the lines around her mouth were harder.

Josephine Hoffman had not yet given up the fight for freedom. She leaned close to DeKok in the small interrogation room.

"They're very suspicious around here," she whispered. "You've got to watch every word you say."

"Is that why you told them you don't have a lover?"

She looked at him, her mouth became harder still.

"I have no lover," she said abruptly, bitingly.

DeKok looked serious.

"You're right," he said brutally, while his hands sought hers. "You're right . . . no lover, not anymore." He felt her hands tighten on his, as if she knew what was coming. "He was killed last night," added DeKok sadly.

Her eyes widened.

"Killed?"

DeKok nodded.

"Yes, Alexander Peetersen . . . murdered . . . in the same way as your husband."

She seemed stunned and for a long time she stared at him without uttering a sound. Then her head dropped toward the table, covering their hands. Her shoulders shook.

DeKok let her be for a while. He felt her tears on his hands. Then he gently removed one of his hands and placed it on her head.

"I understand," he said softly. "After everything you had to endure with Jan-Willem, I understand . . . about Alex."

She raised her head, tears streaming down her face. DeKok felt his hand squeezed with a strength he had not expected of her.

"Alex was a sweet man . . . a dear man . . . soft, considerate, understanding." She closed her eyes and shook her head. "Shot down . . . why?"

DeKok sighed deeply.

"Mrs. Peetersen asked the same question. I could not answer her, either. Not yet. But I promise that . . ."

Josephine interrupted.

"What did she say about me?"

"Who?"

"Mrs. Peetersen."

There was a silence.

"It was not flattering," said DeKok evasively.

"Tell me!"

"Ach, it was in the heat of the moment . . ."

"Tell me! I want to know."

"She . . . eh, she said something about a slut from the streets."

Josephine lowered her head.

"I can understand that," she said softly. Her voice was hoarse. "Thanks for telling me. I don't agree, but I understand it. Mrs. Peetersen is from a totally different environment . . . people with money . . . like Alex . . . like his parents. There is a lot of money . . . in both families."

DeKok put his hand under her chin and gently forced her face up, forced her to look at him. There was a friendly expression on his face.

"Perhaps the money came from robbery, piracy," he said earnestly. "Or the slave trade. Our ancestors were not very picky when it came to making money."

She shrugged her shoulders.

"Father was a burglar. Everybody knew it."

DeKok nodded slowly, keeping eye contact.

"Sure he was . . . the grocer, the butcher, the baker around the corner . . . they all knew how Henkie made his money. But they took it. Nobody said: *I won't sell to you*." He gave her an encouraging pat on the shoulder. "That's the way it is with money, Josephine . . . it doesn't stink . . . not really, no matter what people say."

She pressed her lips together. The fire was back in her eyes.

"As soon as I'm out of here," she said belligerently, "I'll make her eat her words . . . I'll make sure she'll never forget *that slut from the streets*."

"No, you won't," said DeKok. "There's no reason to make her words come true."

He paused to make sure his words penetrated.

"How did you meet Alexander Peetersen?"

"A party with friends."

"Did Jan-Willem and Alex know each other?"

She pulled up one corner of her mouth, the beginning of a smile.

"Well, I never introduced them to each other, as you can well imagine."

"The party . . . was Jan-Willem there as well?"

"No, it was actually the first time I went anywhere on my own."

"So, Alex was not a member of Jan-Willem's circle of acquaintances?"

"No."

"Business relations?"

She hesitated.

"Not as far as I know. I never heard Alex say anything about it."

"About a month before his death Jan-Willem had some suspicions about an affair between you and another man. He discussed it with his parents."

She narrowed her eyes.

"Did he know who it was?"

DeKok shook his head.

"Probably not. In any case, he did not mention a name to his parents. But Mrs. Peetersen knew exactly who was her husband's mistress."

"Yes, I expect so. Alex talked about me to his wife. He told me so."

"Why didn't you tell me you had a lover?"

She stroked her hair. It was a tired gesture.

"I was afraid," she said languidly. "I was afraid that it would later be used against me. I knew very well it could be seen as a motive."

DeKok stood up. He looked down at her.

"Josephine . . . do you have *anything* to do with the death of your husband?"

She looked at him and shook her head.

"No, I swear. I swear on the heads of my children."

DeKok gave her a castigating look.

"There's an old Dutch saying . . . 'who swears easily, lies easily.' "

She scrambled to her feet, a wild look in her eyes. She reached across the table and grabbed DeKok by the lapels of his coat.

"DeKok," she screamed and shook him. "in God's name . . . you *must* believe me!"

7

"And?"

"I'm inclined to believe her."

Vledder shook his head disapprovingly.

"Two murders, two men and both had a relationship with Josephine."

"What are you trying to say?" asked DeKok, grinning. "You're trying to imply that Josephine is some sort of *femme fatale* ... every man who is intimate with her is doomed to death?" He rubbed his chin. "No, I don't believe in that, she's no witch."

"Maybe you're right," shrugged Vledder. "Maybe she's got nothing to do with it. But it *is* strange. The murders are almost identical and it appears that they have been committed by the same person. Really, the only difference, apparent difference, is that the location of the murder is different."

"Did you examine the contents of Jan-Willem's pockets?"

"Yes. He too, had a beautiful, leather-bound pocket agenda."

"Did you take it with you?"

"No, I tried, but Weingarter claimed he needed it for *his* investigation. Besides, there was nothing in it of much interest. I took a photocopy of the more important pages." He paused.

"There was also a street map of Amsterdam among Jan-Willem's belongings."

DeKok looked up.

"New? With a place marked off?"

"Yep. A brand new map. Straight from the store. And the particular gravel path in Rembrandt Park was carefully indicated."

"Does Weingarter have any idea how Jan-Willem came to have that map?"

Vledder stopped in front of a red light.

"No, he didn't follow up on it. He didn't think it was of any importance."

"Not important?"

"No. He figured as follows: Somebody . . . the killer, makes an appointment with his victim, Jan-Willem, and Jan-Willem marks the place for the appointment on a map."

DeKok gestured angrily.

"Did you tell Weingarter that Peetersen had the same kind of map?"

"Sure," nodded Vledder. "According to our colleague that was quite understandable. Rembrandt Park is relatively new . . . it's only been open a few years. Not every Amsterdammer knows where it is. The same goes for the construction site at Lastage Road. There's no . . . eh, no tradition connected with those places."

"Nonsense. The two spots were carefully selected. Very carefully. I'm convinced that the killer simply sent his, or her, victims an invitation."

Vledder was doubtful.

"Complete with a map of Amsterdam, indicating the spot where the deadly confrontation was to take place?"

"The light is green," said DeKok.

* * *

Meindert Post, the Watch Commander, had a voice similar to that of his ancestors, who wrested a living from the treacherous North Sea. Sometimes he sounded like he was standing on the deck of a trawler, trying to make himself heard over a raging storm. Even his normal speaking voice was several decibels louder than the average person.

"DeKok," he roared, "why don't you use your radio? I called Deyssel Street, but you had already left. Your car radio was off, I presume."

"So," said DeKok.

"Well, I told you, I tried to reach you."

"Well, you have. What's so urgent?"

"There's a man waiting for you, upstairs."

"Again?"

"Yes."

"Who?"

Post consulted his notes.

"A Mr. Laar, Hendricus Laar. He says he knows you."

"That's right," said DeKok and turned away toward the stairs leading to the next floor.

On the long bench outside the detective room they found, as expected, Handy Henkie. He looked ill, gray, with rings under his eyes and a stubble on his chin. His clothes looked like he had been sleeping in them. As soon as he saw DeKok, he stood up.

"DeKok," he called out. "It's all wrong this way. Something has to happen, quick. They'll think the child really done it."

DeKok took him by an arm and led the ex-burglar toward his desk.

73

"Here," said DeKok, "have a seat first." Henkie sat down on the edge of his chair. "Did you know," continued DeKok, "that Josephine had a lover?"

"Of course I knowed," was the tired reply. "That's got nothing to do with it."

"Alexander Peetersen was murdered."

"Accident."

DeKok shook his head.

"Both murders were carefully planned."

Henkie sighed deeply.

"I mean ... it's an accident that the victim were Alex, a man who had an affair with my Josephine. You see, the relationship got nothing to do with the motive."

"Then ... what's the motive?"

"Come now, DeKok," said Henkie, raising his arms and shrugging his shoulders at the same time, "... if I knew that, I'd tell you. That child has to come out of jail. She's gonna die in that cell. She's not like me ... she can't do time."

"Where is Red Bakker?"

Henkie closed his eyes and shook his head.

"I don't know ... I don't know. I've gone everywhere, asked everybody. It's as if he's gone ... gone from the face of the earth."

"Red lives off blackmail." It was not a question.

"Sure, makes no sense to deny it ... not to you."

"Do you know any of his ... eh, contributors?"

"Of course not." Henkie shook his head with irritation.

"Do you know if they include anybody from among Jan-Willem's circle of friends? Or Alex Peetersen's?"

"Never heard anything like that."

"Did Red Bakker know about the relationship between Josephine and Alex?"

"Maybe," said Henkie with a dull voice. "But ... he wouldn't never have *dared* to ..."

DeKok raised his hands in protest.

"He had enough nerve to propose a murder to Josephine ... and he had enough nerve to tell Jan-Willem's parents an interesting story about your daughter."

Vledder watched attentively as Henkie seemed to be transformed into a small, compact package of hate. Henkie pressed his lips together and gave DeKok a look from steel-blue eyes that would have melted metal.

"You can be sure, DeKok," said Josephine's father, "that was the last story Red Bakker told in his life."

He stood up and calmly walked away, without acknowledging either of the Inspectors. One of the detectives nearer the door looked a question at DeKok. DeKok shook his head and smiled. Henkie slammed the door behind him.

* * *

"How's it going?"

Vledder studied his computer terminal.

"I entered everything I could think of ... height, weight, age, profession, interests, social contacts, you name it. But I can't find any similarities between the two victims, other than the way they were killed. Maybe you can say that both were 'comfortable,' as rich people like to say when they speak about money. But that's about it."

"And yet," said DeKok, "they were both killed by the same person."

"Exactly. And that's what's so intriguing. If we ignore, for the moment, the three we know about, that is Red Bakker, Handy Henkie and Josephine ... we almost *have* to concentrate on somebody who knew *both* victims, *without* knowing any of the first three. There may be a number of unknowns."

"Unknowns," grinned DeKok. "I like that. It may be the soundest opinion you've had in months."

"What a rotten thing to say." Vledder made a threatening gesture. "It's a good thing I have such a respect for your advanced age. If you were younger, I'd ask you to step outside with me."

"Don't let my gray hairs stop you," said DeKok nonchalantly. "I've known some of the greatest street fighters of all time: Tony Canal, he always dropped his victims in the nearest canal, whether they could swim, or not. There was Herring Artie, Buck Jones, Rotterdam Knocker ... people who, in their hey days, made life on the Seadike ... interesting. I have not forgotten everything I learned during those days. In those days," DeKok continued to reminisce, "we only had the saber and were expected to keep order. You could only do that if you proved to be the better man."

"Rotterdam Knocker?" asked Vledder, interested despite himself.

"Yes, they called him that because when he hit you, you'd think you were in Rotterdam when you came to. I remember . . ."

Aad Ishoven, the wizard of the administrative staff at Warmoes Street, interrupted. He stood in front of DeKok's desk and slapped a folder in front of the gray sleuth.

"I found it," he announced.

"What?"

"I thought it was important," said Aad, a disappointed tone in his voice. "You made such a noise about it. Poor Frans was upset for hours."

"Ah," said DeKok, "that was because I seemed to remember having seen Jan-Willem Hoffman in the station at one time or another."

"That's right."

"What's right?"

"You are and he was. Jan-Willem Hoffman is in our records."

"Really, how?"

Ishoven pointed at the folder.

"Frans was looking among the suspects that went through here and indeed, he's not listed there." He looked at DeKok and gave him a wink. "Because I didn't want to damage your reputation for remembering faces, I did a global search and found him. Jan-Willem Hoffman was in the station, not as a suspect, but as a complainant."

"Complainant of what?"

Ishoven picked up the folder and searched through it.

"It's a bit strange," he began. "Jan-Willem Hoffman came to the station last August, in the middle of the night, around three in the morning, actually. He told the Watch Commander that he wanted to file a complaint pertaining to blackmail. The Watch Commander noted name, date of birth and that sort of thing in the log. Well, you know how it is, downstairs, they never have time to log it properly, in the computer. Especially some of the older men still use the old-fashioned journals and . . ."

"Yes, yes," interrupted DeKok, who wholeheartedly approved of the old-fashioned journals and despised the computers, "go on."

"Well, they wrote it in the log and told Hoffman to come back in the morning to talk to a detective. There were none in the station at that time."

"Did he show up?"

"That's just it. He didn't. By the time they got around to entering the paper log into the computer, several days had gone by and they noticed there was no follow-up. Kamphouse then

77

gave the information to Inspector Riggelink with instructions to interview Hoffman."

"And that happened?"

"Yes, I think. Riggelink sent Hoffman a letter with the request to come to the station so the complaint could be formalized. According to the paper work, Hoffman did indeed come to the station and that's when you must have seen him."

DeKok stared into the distance for several long seconds.

"What happened to the complaint?"

"Nothing," said Ishoven. "Here's the report." DeKok waved it away, so Ishoven continued. "It's only about half a page long. According to Riggelink, Hoffman said that the situation had changed and he was no longer interested in filing a complaint, or having an investigation instituted. Riggelink assured him that everything was in confidence, that he could count on the utmost discretion from the police ... but to no avail."

DeKok nodded his understanding.

"And that was it. There never was a case." He looked at Vledder. "How come you didn't find that in your magic box?" he asked.

While Ishoven had been talking, Vledder had been busy at his terminal.

"I made the same mistake as Frans," said Vledder. "I looked in the wrong files. But it won't happen again, I'll make sure to cross-reference them from now on. Don't really know why I didn't do that before. It's such an obvious thing to do. I can probably tap into Headquarters and ..."

DeKok held up his hands in surrender.

"Spare me," he said, "I could care less how you do it. Thank God there are still back-up files in paper and," he smiled at Ishoven, "thank God there are still administrators who don't stare themselves blind at a TV screen. Thanks, Aad," he added,

"I really appreciate it and I always knew you'd come through in the end."

Aad Ishoven was flattered and left. DeKok turned toward Vledder.

"Well?"

Vledder looked at his screen before he answered.

"Nothing else, really. There was nothing in the report about blackmail. Since Hoffman didn't want to press charges, there was nothing to say. All we have is the original entry in the log."

"That's not much help," grumbled DeKok. "Well, at least we know that at one time Jan-Willem Hoffman was in some way involved with blackmail."

"Red Bakker?"

DeKok placed his feet on the desk and with a pained expression rubbed his calves. It felt as if a thousand devils poked his legs with red-hot pitchforks. The pain was almost unbearable and usually happened when a case was not progressing smoothly. Whenever he was going in the wrong direction, was getting further and further away from the solution, his legs and his feet would hurt. His mind knew it was purely psychosomatic, but his body belied the imaginary nature of the discomfort. Just because the pain is psychosomatic, he thought, doesn't make it any less real.

Vledder was well acquainted with the symptoms.

"Tired feet?" he asked anxiously.

DeKok nodded and closed his eyes. He remained that way for several minutes, fighting the pain. His face resembled a steel mask and Vledder imagined he could hear the grinding of DeKok's teeth.

Finally, with an effort, DeKok placed his feet back on the floor and stood up.

"Come on," he said to Vledder.

"Where to?"

"To Lowee's . . . only cognac can save me now."

8

They ambled through the Red Light District, or the Quarter, as it is called by the natives. It was busy. The wind of the last few days had died down considerably and soft, spring-like weather had enticed people from their houses. The crowds were gathered in front of the sex-cinemas: nervous, loud Germans, smaller, delicately featured Moroccans, Turkish guest-workers and a few, quiet Dutchmen. The scatological display windows of the sex-shops attracted their share of the prurient. Shreds of popular music thundered from open bar doors and through it all wafted the unmistakable odor of Amsterdam's inner city: a melange of dozens of food aromas, mixed with the smell of stale beer and the occasional whiff of perfume.

A young, wandering heroin-prostitute stumbled through the crowds and next to the cigarette machine stood a tall black man, leaning against the facade. Strong, white teeth gleamed in a dark face of classical beauty while he casually cleaned his finger nails with a long switchblade and his eyes roamed the crowds with a calculating look.

DeKok was very familiar with the scene, his entire police career had been in and around the Quarter. He knew most of the regular inhabitants by face and a large percentage by name and nickname. The scene had changed over the years. The cozy, easy-going world of the professional prostitute was changing into a criminal jungle where the police were barely able to hold their own. It was why Warmoes Street Station was considered to be the busiest police station in Europe and was often referred to as the Dutch "Hill Street" ever since the popular American TV series had been shown on Dutch TV.

The current, rather weak city government practiced an administration of excessive tolerance which was in the process of transforming Amsterdam into an open city where everything was allowed. The results were inevitable. The "fame" soon spread across the borders and, attracted by a tolerant application of the Criminal Code, criminals from all over the world gathered in Amsterdam . . . Mafia representatives from Italy, robbers and extortionists from the former Yugoslavia, purse snatchers and pickpockets from South America and drug dealers from as far away as Hong Kong and Singapore. Amsterdam, which carried the word "merciful" in its Coat of Arms, had become a cosmopolitan meeting place for international crime.*

DeKok observed it all with sad eyes and a silent melancholy for the "good old days" when Amsterdam was still the "fun city" of Europe, according to many travel experts. He did not feel responsible for the moral weakening of the people, or the degeneration of the city he loved. No matter in what low esteem the concept "justice" had been held, he had served it to the best of his abilities.

He pressed his lips together. He would *not* capitulate. Never. And to be honest, he thought, there are already noticeable signs that things were improving. Drug use was down fifty percent and the number of dealers had rapidly dwindled in the last few years. By decriminalizing the softer drugs and making

---

* Underneath the Coat of Arms of Amsterdam, and an integral part of it, are the words *heroic, resolute and merciful.*

other drugs available through state-run "drug" stores, the profit motive had been severely curtailed. Every year fewer young girls were being enslaved by the drugs and this reduced the number of "heroin whores" who were looked down upon by the "professionals." A young girl in need of a fix would do anything, including having sex without a condom and, greatest sin of all in the eyes of the Dutch, cut her prices.

DeKok approved of prostitution. He did not approve of pimps, or those who exploited the women. But he felt strongly that prostitution made it possible for "honest" women to walk the streets in relative safety. Rape is a rare, and unusually severely punished crime in the Netherlands.

Vledder had his own thoughts. He, too, knew about the past of the Quarter and he knew DeKok. Vledder sometimes looked upon DeKok as a Don Quixote who fought the windmills of crime, indifference and injustice with his lance of righteous indignation against the perpetrators and with infinite compassion for the victims. Vledder stopped short of comparing himself to Sancho Panza.

Yes, thought Vledder and DeKok, almost simultaneously, Amsterdam has changed, but it will always be the same, it will always be Amsterdam.

Suddenly they saw Fred Prins, further down the street. The young Inspector moved unsteadily in their direction. DeKok tapped Vledder's shoulder.

"There's Fred. Have you heard from him yet?"

"No, I haven't spoken to him since this morning."

DeKok looked at his watch.

"It's almost nine o'clock. Has he been on the case all this time?"

Vledder laughed.

"Well, it seems that he may have been delayed somewhat by the proverbial hospitality of our Chinese friends." He looked at DeKok, who had a well-known weakness for Oriental food. "You know how it goes ... a nice little *babi pangang* with a Heineken or two and maybe a cognac as dessert."

Fred Prins had not noticed them. He walked with his head down and when he was about to pass them by without seeing them, DeKok took him by the arm. The young Inspector looked up in surprise. He looked at DeKok with open mouth and a sheepish expression on his face. Then came recognition.

"Well, I'll be," he said, "the old man himself. I had not expected that. You're still out late."

"The same can be said to you, my fine feathered Prins," said DeKok jovially.

"Well, yes ..."

"Find out anything?" asked Vledder quickly.

"Yes." Prins gave Vledder a grateful look. "Alexander Peetersen was in *Lotus*, a Chinese Restaurant on Bantam Street. According to my information he arrived there about quarter past eight and left close to ten in the evening."

"Was he alone?"

Fred Prins closed his eyes and shook his head, as if to clear his thoughts.

"Well, you see, DeKok, I wanted to do as thorough a job as possible. By around noon I already knew that Peetersen had dined in the *Lotus*. But the owner didn't know all the details. He remembered that Peetersen was in company with a tall, skinny guy. He even knew what table they had used. A bit separated, on an elevated part of the floor, behind a low railing. He advised me to wait for Sita."

"Who's Sita?"

"A Chinese girl. She waited on that particular table that night."

"And you went to look for her?"

Prins looked apologetic.

"No, I didn't go looking for her. That would have been nonproductive. I didn't have a clue about her whereabouts and the owner didn't know where she lives. At least, that's what he said. I had no address, no phone number . . . nothing. Not even a last name. All he knew was that she'd be back around six." He paused momentarily. "I didn't feel much like hanging around that restaurant, so I went to work on another case, one I've been assigned to. And around six I went back to the *Lotus*."

"And?"

Fred stepped out of the main stream of people and leaned against a nearby facade. He found his notebook and started to read, editing as he went.

"Sita spoke excellent Dutch," he began. "She lives with her parents and has been in Amsterdam for some time. She immediately recognized Peetersen from the photo I showed her. Although the picture is clearly the photograph of a dead man, she did not comment on it."

"Strange."

Prins shrugged his shoulders.

"Perhaps I misinterpreted her reactions. The inscrutable Orient and all that."

"And what about the skinny man?"

"She thought he was about fifty years old, but added almost immediately that she had trouble with the ages of white people." He grinned brightly. "According to Sita *we* have inscrutable faces."

"Could she give you a description?"

"Oh, yes. An excellent description, as a matter of fact. Useful, anyway. She thought he was about six feet tall with a narrow, thin face and thin lips. Short, gray hair with a little bit of a wave. According to Sita he was a real gentleman, distinguished, well dressed and with an aristocratic accent."

"Aristocratic, what does that mean?"

"Well, you know, as if they have a hot potato in their mouth when they talk."

"All right," growled DeKok, who was a confirmed egalitarian, "go on."

"Well, although I didn't have much hope, I asked Sita to accompany me to the station. The restaurant owner was upset about it, but she agreed. She looked at our picture gallery, but did not recognize him. He may not be in it, you know."

DeKok looked pensively at the throngs that swirled around their little group.

"Did she remember any names? For instance, how did they address each other?"

"No, nothing."

"Did either say anything particular?"

Prins put his notebook back in his pocket and spread his hands.

"Apparently, based on the gesticulations, they had a lively conversation. But Sita didn't hear a thing. Whenever she was near the table, they fell silent. Even when she asked the usual question, if the meal was all right, they didn't answer."

"Did they leave at the same time?"

"No. They also did not arrive at the same time. Peetersen was first and he was the first to leave. The long, skinny man left about ten minutes later."

"Were they regular visitors?"

"Sita said she had never seen them before and they were strangers to the owner as well."

DeKok smiled at Prins.

"Good work," he said. Then he leaned closer to the young Inspector and smelled his breath.

"Courvoisier?"

"How did you guess?"

"Ah, a well developed nose for the noblest beverage of them all, my boy."

* * *

Lowee, because of his small stature, known as Little Lowee, greeted both Inspectors heartily.

"Well, well, well," he exclaimed, rubbing his hands. "I's glad to see you again." He looked at DeKok with a happy expression on his small, mousey face. "Everything hunky-dory? You been gone so long I were just about to come to the station, meself."

DeKok grinned.

"Why, to give yourself up?"

Lowee looked offended.

"Give meself up?" he exclaimed with the voice of a martyr. He thumped his chest. "Whadda I ever done to give meself up for." He made a violent gesture with the rag he used to wipe off the bar. "I was just worried, is all. There's so many crazies around with heaters, datta, I . . . eh, . . ."

DeKok interrupted with a smile.

"You were afraid they'd shot *me*?"

Lowee spread his arms.

"I tole you . . . they're crazy. Espectacally them H-junkies. Iffen they think you got as much as a dime, you're a goner, and tha's for sure." he turned toward Vledder. "H is heroin," he explained with a supercilious smile.

Vledder nodded calmly. He was used to being just barely tolerated by Lowee. DeKok was Lowee's friend, but Vledder was just another cop.

"They come here at all?" asked DeKok.

87

"Aw, come on, DeKok. Sometime they does. But I ain't blind, you knows. I spot them rightaway. Iffen they spent too much time inna can . . ."

"Shooting up?"

Lowee nodded seriously.

"Sometime, I tell ya . . . blood onna walls, them needles behind the stool." He leaned forward. "Well, you see, the real heroin-whores is known. They don't get inna door, nomore. I cain't have that. I'll get all sorta trouble witta me regulars, you see. The pros. Them Heroin-kids are bad for business. They don't care. And they *steal*." The last word was said with real indignation. DeKok smiled inwardly, but nodded seriously. Lowee was known to be a fence on the side, although he had never been caught. "Oh, yes," added Lowee, warming to his subject. "They'll ruin the perfession, you knows. I means to say, iffen a john gets robbed by one of them junkies, he won't come back to give the business to a *respectable*, working girl. Stand to reason, donit?"

DeKok nodded.

"That's why there is all them clubs, nowadays," continued Lowee, "it's safer, they think. And the bordellos all over town. "Heck," he added, well aware of DeKok's aversion to strong language, "before you knows it the Quarter is done spread all over the city."

DeKok gave a meaningful look at the empty bar top in front of him. Lowee took the hint.

"Ah well," said the barkeeper, "enough of that, already. Let me pour you a good one."

He dove underneath the bar and emerged almost immediately with three large snifters and a bottle of excellent cognac, kept there especially for DeKok's visits. He poured with a generous hand and then waited for the others to lift their glasses.

"*Proost*," said Lowee.

"To the respectability of the Quarter," added DeKok.

"Amen," agreed Lowee.

Vledder, as usual, remained silent.

DeKok took his first, careful sip and then held the glass cradled in his hand. Slowly he rocked the glass back and forth and a look of pure delight transformed his face. Carefully he took another sip and allowed the amber liquid to glide down his appreciative throat. Then, eyes closed with enjoyment, he nodded in Lowee's direction.

"You know, Lowee, the old Greeks had a god who was liked by all, without exception."

"That ain't possible," challenged Lowee.

DeKok nodded convincingly.

"Oh, yes, it is . . . Bacchus."

Lowee laughed out loud.

"I don't think we gotta God that loves booze. Sometimes they come here from the Salvation Army, you knows, well iffen you listen to them . . ."

The gray sleuth cradled his glass with both hands and carefully replaced it on the bar counter. It was a tender, almost reverential movement. DeKok loved cognac and enjoyed intensely the moments when he could indulge his passion in the cozy, half-dark bar of his friend, Little Lowee.

"I don't know," said DeKok hesitantly, "if they're right. If He had not wanted us to drink . . . He would never have given us the vines. He must know us mortals well enough to know we can't resist." He pushed his glass closer to Lowee. "Pour again, my diminutive friend."

Lowee obeyed with the speed and dedication of a good publican.

"You're looking for Red Bakker, ain't you?" he asked suddenly.

"Says who?" asked DeKok wearily.

"Well, I hears this and that."

"Who from?"

"Everybody . . . all them working girls, them wise guys, even them pimps wanna know about Red. Handy Henkie is after it, of course. They whispers that he's willing to pay for the info."

"And?"

"Iffen you asks me, they's never gonna find him. Red's in Spain, atta Costa Brava, or them Canary Islands."

"Why do you say that?"

Lowee looked around surreptitiously and then leaned closer.

"Red Bakker has a thing with Black Judy, you knows, her from Old Acquaintance Alley. Well, she was here too, you knows, and she gets a few down and she starts talking . . . about da business and about Red Bakker who's gonna make a big haul real soon."

"A big haul?"

"Yessir, he done told her he's found a little gold-mine. It was justa matter of getting the geezer to pay up."

"What geezer?"

Lowee grinned.

"Well, DeKok, iffen I knows *that*, Red woulda been in the clink and it woulda be me at the Costa Brava."

9

Vledder paced agitatedly back and forth in front of DeKok's desk. His face was red.

"I could care less," he said passionately. "So what if Red Bakker made some sort of big haul. I don't envy him his little vacation at the Costa Brava. As far as I'm concerned, he's got nothing to do with the case we're handling." He stopped suddenly in front of DeKok's desk. "I'm much more interested in that tall, skinny guy who dined with Peetersen, just before he died. Could he be the killer?"

DeKok showed a certain hesitation.

"Theoretically it's always possible, of course. He could be the one who directed Peetersen to Lastage Road and then killed him. He was around at the right time and in the right neighborhood. Opportunity of time and place, so to speak. Let's assume the meeting was arranged for ten o'clock. After Peetersen left, the skinny man could easily arrive at the place. And . . . it's happened before that a killer allowed himself the macabre pleasure of inviting his intended victim to a last meal . . ."

"So," prompted Vledder.

"If the skinny man is the killer, it's almost certain that Peetersen had no idea about the identity of his killer. It's absurd to assume that he would first have an elaborate meal with the man and then make an appointment to meet him, almost immediately afterwards, at a deserted spot."

Vledder was perplexed.

"Is it possible that Peetersen and Hoffman *knew* their killer?"

DeKok did not answer. He rummaged in his desk drawer and found a bag of hard candy. He stared into the bag for almost a minute, before he made a selection. Then he put the bag back in his desk.

"We finally received the official report from the weapons expert," said DeKok. "It's now an official fact that both men were killed with the same weapon. And ... in view of the location and grouping of the shots, we can safely assume that the shots were all fired by the same person." He tapped his desk. "Therefore we are *certain* that there was a perpetrator. If that seems obvious to you, consider that there seems to be no connection. Why did the victims fall for the invitation from the killer? What sort of power did the killer have to enable him, or her, to direct the victims to those deserted places. Did they have any idea about the danger they were facing? Or were both completely oblivious and no more than sheep led to slaughter?"

"Well," said Vledder, "if you reason that way, we can also reason in reverse. Why did the killer select *these* two victims? What was the motive? Were they in the way, somehow? Were they a threat to the killer?"

DeKok made a helpless gesture, sucking on his candy.

"Those are all questions we can't answer," he admitted sadly. "I have the uncomfortable feeling we're just at the beginning ... that the end of this affair is a long way out of sight."

Vledder was shocked.

"Do you seriously mean that there will be more victims? That there will be more killings?"

"Possibly. As long as we're in the dark about the background, nothing is impossible."

They fell silent. Vledder sank down on the corner of DeKok's desk. A defective ballast in the fluorescent light fixture hummed annoyingly. The usual noise and clatter of the detective room washed around them. DeKok stared up at the ceiling. A heavy, wooden support beam was cracked. This old station should just collapse, he thought. Warmoes Street has always been a factory for processing misery and crime.

Vledder finally broke the silence. He held a finger in the air.

"If the tall, skinny guy is *not* the killer, it's just possible that Peetersen discussed his upcoming meeting with him?"

DeKok grimaced.

"I'd like to talk to him myself. Perhaps he can provide us with a lead."

"If only we knew who he is."

"Yes, that, as they say, is it in a nutshell. In any case, our skinny friend is not exactly guarding his anonymity. While the killer prefers dark, secretive places for his meetings, the skinny man has dinner in a public restaurant."

"Well," smiled Vledder, "maybe he's got nothing to hide."

"Exactly. He's not secretive. We should be able to establish the identity of this man. Why don't you give the description to Weingarter at Deyssel Street. He can ask Josephine if she recognizes him at all."

Vledder looked confuse.

"But the skinny man dined with Peetersen, not with Hoffman."

"Yes, but Josephine was a . . . a *friend* of Peetersen. An intimate friend. Surely she must know *some* people from his environment." He slapped a flat hand in the desk. "I'm looking for connections, similarities . . . similarities between the victims. Any similarities at all." He gestured toward Vledder. "Speaking about similarities, have you compared the beautiful pocket agendas of both gentlemen?"

"Yes, I did . . . nothing there."

"What about the phone numbers?"

"What do you mean?"

DeKok reacted impatiently.

"The usual phone numbers in an agenda . . . was there a common number? I mean a phone number that both had noted down?"

Vledder nodded slowly as he moved in front of his terminal. He struck a number of keys and then stared at the screen.

"Yes," he said. "There was such a number. Here it is . . . 299-0216, here in Amsterdam."

DeKok suddenly sat up straight.

"Why didn't you tell me?"

"Because it's nothing," said Vledder, shrugging his shoulders.

"What nothing?"

Vledder shook his head.

"Of course, I checked it out, what do you think? It's the phone number of a psychiatrist . . . a Doctor Beaumonde, at Emperors Canal."

"And?"

"The man has been dead for five years."

* * *

Commissaris* Buitendam, the tall, stately chief of Warmoes Street police station, waved a slender hand at Dekok and invited him to sit down.

"I'd rather stand," said DeKok.

"Please yourself," said his Chief curtly. He was visibly nervous as he rummaged through his desk and read a note. "Commissaris Dietinga, Chief of the Deyssel Street station, approached me this morning. He was extremely displeased. According to him, the cooperation and coordination between his station and you leaves much to be desired."

DeKok did not seem surprised. He smiled gently.

"Strange opinions, for a Commissaris," said DeKok, grinning.

Buitendam ignored the remark.

"Dietinga," continued the Commissaris in his affected voice, "is under the impression that you have neglected to share information with his detective team. Therefore it's extremely difficult for his detectives to continue the investigation in the murders."

DeKok shook his head.

"Nonsense."

Buitendam's pale face reddened.

"A Commissaris," he barked indignantly, "does not speak nonsense."

DeKok laughed.

"All right, then. Double talk, gibberish, blather, gobbledy-gook, drivel, balderdash, malarkey and bunk . . . call it what you will . . . any way you slice it, it's obvious . . . they are not getting

* Commissaris: a rank equivalent to Captain. There are only two ranks higher: Chief-Commissaris and Chief Constable. Each jurisdiction has only a single Chief Constable, the highest possible police rank. There is one Chief Constable for all of Amsterdam. Other ranks in the Municipal Police are: Constable, Constable First Class, Sergeant, Adjutant, Inspector, Chief-Inspector and Commissaris. Adjutants and below are equivalent to non-commissioned ranks. Inspector is a rank equivalent to 2nd Lieutenant.

any results. And who's fault is that?" DeKok's tone was ironic. "Aha, of course, it's got to be DeKok! He's withholding information!" DeKok shook his head. "They were a little bit too fast off the mark and arrested Josephine Hoffman too quickly. Their first mistake."

Buitendam gestured violently, slapped the top of his desk.

"The arrest of that woman was with the full approval of the Judge-Advocate."

DeKok smiled contemptuously.

"Ach," he said. "What does a man like that know? After all, he has to go by what other people tell him. Perhaps he knows how to write up an indictment, give a summation and otherwise make himself useful in front of a bunch of judges who also have never walked the streets . . . But *investigation*, the real detective work, *that* is something the Judge-Advocate knows nothing about." He nodded encouragingly in his Chief's direction. "The best thing they can do at Deyssel Street is let Josephine go as soon as possible. Holding her was their second mistake."

"That's none of your business."

DeKok nodded calmly, irritatingly.

"That's right . . . that has to be decided by the Judge-Advocate."

Again Buitendam slapped the top of his desk.

"Yes, the Judge-Advocate, the principal investigating officer."

DeKok shrugged his shoulders, a bored look on his face.

"Yes, yes, according to the Law. And perhaps it *should* be that way. But in practice it just doesn't work. I mean, what does that man do with all his responsibilities and powers?" DeKok snorted. "Sits in an office all day and reads reports. He'd be better off transferring his authority to the cop in the street, the one who does the actual work."

DeKok had said enough. He turned around and walked away.

The Commissaris called him back.

"You're to take the entire case," he roared. "The murder in Rembrandt Park too."

DeKok sighed deeply.

"I was afraid that was what all this song-and-dance was leading up to," he said resignedly. "There is one condition."

"And that is?"

"Josephine Haar will immediately be set free."

Commissaris Buitendam swallowed.

"That . . . that . . ." he stammered.

DeKok smiled benignly and looked him straight in the eyes.

". . . will be taken care of immediately," completed Buitendam.

"You see," said DeKok amiably. "That wasn't so hard."

Buitendam came around his desk, waved his arms in the air and then pointed at the door.

"OUT!" he roared.

DeKok left.

* * *

Vledder laughed.

"You're incorrigible. If Commissaris Buitendam ever dies of a heart attack, I'll have to arrest you for murder."

DeKok shrugged that danger into oblivion.

"Deyssel Street apparently sees no way out. Small wonder . . . by arresting Josephine they put all their eggs in one basket and now they're stuck. Commissaris Dietinga over there has managed to get Buitendam crazy enough to take over the entire case, both murders."

"Oh, yes? Well, take it from me, that didn't take a lot of persuading. Buitendam likes to brag about his 'ace-detective' all the time. I would be surprised if the initial suggestion didn't come from our own, esteemed Chief."

"Whatever," said DeKok easily. "But," he went on, "it would be best if you go over to Deyssel Street and gather up anything they have on Hoffman and bring it back." He rubbed the bridge of his nose with a little finger. "And bring back Josephine as well."

Vledder looked surprised.

"You want to lock her up here?"

DeKok shook his head, contemplating his little finger.

"No, no . . . I want to let her go. It was my only condition."

"And are they going to let you?"

DeKok rubbed his chin.

"Well, it doesn't really matter. If they hand the Hoffman case over to us, Josephine automatically becomes *our* arrestee . . . and I see no grounds for holding her in custody any longer."

"Buitendam was pretty pis . . . eh, upset. What if he doesn't go along?"

"Then," DeKok said grimly, "I'll whisper something in the ear of her lawyer."

Vledder rubbed his hands.

"I'm starting to want to go on again," he smirked. He opened a desk drawer and pulled something out. "The map that was found with Peetersen," he explained, holding it up in the air. "I checked with the publisher. Just in Amsterdam there are twenty-seven stores that sell this map. Then, of course, there are points of sale in Rotterdam, The Hague . . . all the big cities. And at news stands and tourist shops. It's impossible to get any leads through this."

"What about the phone numbers?"

"From the dead psychiatrist?"

"From the dead psychiatrist," repeated DeKok.

Vledder looked puzzled.

"What about it?"

DeKok pursed his lips.

"Well," he said pensively, "this about it: Why would two people have gone to the trouble to write a phone number in their brand new, expensive agenda? A phone number of a man who's been dead for five years?"

Vledder's face fell.

"That's strange, indeed. I never thought about that."

DeKok spread his hands and pursued his own question.

"To call a dead man? To call him in the hereafter?"

He stared into the distance, deep in thought. His brain sometimes worked in mysterious ways and a sinister thought came to the surface. It bothered him, frightened him a little. He rubbed dry lips with the back of his hands.

"A phone call," he said hoarsely, ". . . a phone call to the hereafter."

10

With outstretched hands, DeKok walked toward Josephine. He put his arms around her and hugged her briefly.

"I'm glad you're free again," he whispered in her ear. Then he let her go. There were tears in her eyes when she looked at him.

"It was terrible. I didn't know what was going on, what was happening to me, how long it would last. The uncertainty was driving me crazy." She looked around the room, as if searching for someone. "Did they find Red Bakker yet?"

DeKok shook his head.

"Not yet. But don't worry about that. I'm sure he'll retract the damaging remarks he made to Jan-Willem's parents." He led her to the chair next to his desk. "Red Bakker's statement and the fact that there was a motive led to your arrest."

"And that is no longer so?"

"Nothing has changed," smiled DeKok. "But Deyssel Street has turned the case over to me, to us, Vledder and me. The complete case, including the suspect. And for me . . . the basis for an arrest is just too tenuous."

"You believe I'm innocent?"

DeKok rubbed the bridge of his nose with a little finger.

"Well, I," he hesitated, "I don't see enough indications of guilt."

"Isn't that the same?"

DeKok was reticent.

"It's a different way of thinking." Then he pointed at her and gave her a winning smile. "Don't worry about it, Josephine. It serves no purpose. We just have to make sure that the real killer is found as soon as possible. *That* is important . . . for you . . . for me . . . for all of us. That is the only way we can effectively clear your name. But you have to help me."

"How . . . with what?"

"Do you know," asked DeKok, "a tall, skinny man of around fifty?"

"Should I?"

"A distinguished man who speaks very la-di-da. He has short, graying hair."

She shook her head slowly.

"It doesn't ring a bell."

"Alex Peetersen had dinner with him on the night he died. They were in a Chinese restaurant at Bantam Street. Ten minutes before he died, Alex had said good bye to him and left the restaurant."

She looked at him with big eyes.

"Is he the killer?"

DeKok shrugged.

"I don't exclude him. But primarily I want to know who he is."

"Was he one of Alex's friends?"

DeKok smiled.

"That's what I'm asking you."

"I'm sorry. I don't know anybody who answers to that description. As far as I know, I've never met the man."

"How about in connection with Jan-Willem?"

She shook her head unhappily.

"You must keep in mind that I only played a minor role in the life of both men. Jan-Willem was my husband, but there was no question of a real bond, such as with my parents. My relationship with Alex wasn't very deep, either. It was superficial, romantic. Little more than an escape from a failed marriage." She sounded bitter. "So far I've not been lucky in my relationships with men."

"Third time is the charm," DeKok assured her.

She shook her head resolutely.

"No third man in *my* life."

"You're still young, Josephine, and good-looking. Once this nightmare is over ..." He did not finish the sentence. A sudden thought had struck him. "Did Jan-Willem consult a doctor? A doctor Beaumonde?"

There was a guarded look in her eyes.

"Doctor Beaumonde?" she repeated evenly.

"A psychiatrist," prompted DeKok.

Josephine stared past him, out the window, at the blue sky over the rooftops of Warmoes Street. Slowly her gaze returned to him.

"How did you know that?" she asked softly.

"Never mind," said DeKok. "Did he consult him? Was he under treatment?"

She nodded slowly, reluctantly.

"Years ago."

"What for?"

"I don't know," she said. "Jan-Willem never told me anything about it. Apparently it had something to do with an incident that happened before we were married. When he was still a teenager. Some kind of traumatic neurosis, I think." She made an contrite gesture. "At times I related it to his often disinterested attitude toward me."

DeKok was confused and looked it.

"A trauma? What sort of trauma?"

She avoided looking at him. She was obviously troubled by the memories. Her tongue flicked out and wetted her lips.

"Jan-Willem ... he ... Jan-Willem is supposed to have raped a young girl."

DeKok sat back in his chair. Stunned. Not too long ago he and Vledder had solved a case of serial killings that had rape as the root cause. And now he was again confronted with rape. It is an unusual crime in the Netherlands, where prostitutes are readily available. He needed a few moments to collect himself.

He looked at her searchingly.

"Rape?" he asked, disbelief in his voice.

She nodded, her head down.

"That was being whispered. The Hoffmans never did tell me the details. All of it was always very secretive. But I did understand that the affair was settled with the family of the girl. They were bought off. There was never any police involvement. Everything was hushed up."

"And the girl?"

Josephine lifted her head and looked him in the face. Her face was pale and her lips quivered.

"In Arnhem ... in an institution. She never got over it."

* * *

They walked from Old Bridge Alley toward New Maelstrom and went left onto Front Fort Canal. Vledder turned to DeKok.

"How can a simple rape have such terrible consequences that the victim has to be cared for in an institution for the rest of her life?"

DeKok looked at him sternly.

"Apparently you belong to the category of cops who don't take the rape of a woman very seriously. You better believe me, rape is one of the vilest crimes I know and it is *never* simple."

Vledder was getting agitated.

"That's not what I meant at all. I certainly did not intend to think about it as *simple*. But usually the consequences are manageable."

"Exactly . . . manageable. But at what cost? Rape is an invasion of the woman's body *and* soul. It will, without exception, leave permanent scars. Often physical, but always psychological. It is one of the most severely punished crimes in Holland . . . and for a reason. A murderer kills his, or her, victim and the victim is forever beyond human concerns. A thief steals something of value, but it can usually be replaced. But rape robs a woman of her dignity, forces her to submit to an act that should be reserved for her own, private decisions with a person, or persons, of *her* choice. She's forced to live with it. It ruins the rest of her life, most certainly it will forever after affect all her dealings with other people. Some become zombies, some need psychiatric care for the rest of their lives, some kill themselves afterward."

Vledder was properly abashed. Of course, as a cop, he considered rape a crime, but he had never heard such an impassioned plea against rape.

"I'm sorry," said Vledder, "I spoke thoughtlessly and I didn't mean to defend my insensitivity. But what about Jan-Willem?"

"We don't know exactly what happened years ago. Perhaps Jan-Willem used so much force that the physical attack caused brain damage, a knock on the head, for instance. He was a powerfully built man. Perhaps the victim was already mentally impaired before the attack, which would make the crime even more reprehensible if such a thing is possible. However, we don't have enough details. Apparently Jan-Willem didn't escape entirely unscathed himself."

"You mean it traumatized him as well so that years later he still needed treatment by a psychiatrist?"

"Exactly."

"Well, that's too bad, but I can't feel too sorry for him."

DeKok did not answer.

They crossed the street in front of the Royal Palace and passed the imposing new Post Office toward Town Hall Street. Vledder remained quiet for a long time. Finally he spoke up.

"Are you going to dig into that rape case?"

"As much as possible," said DeKok. "Apparently there is no paper work and the Hoffmans will be less than forthcoming in discussing it."

"It could be a motive for murder."

"Yes, but it doesn't fit in with Peetersen."

"How do you mean?"

"There's no mention of rape in his case."

"We don't know that," countered Vledder.

DeKok pursed his lips and shook his head.

"He's more a man for financial dealings, frauds, what have you."

"What does *that* have to do with anything?"

The gray sleuth adjusted his ridiculous little hat and turned right onto Emperors Canal. Vledder, who at first had proceeded straight ahead, caught up with his older partner.

"I asked what that had to do with anything," he repeated, irked.

DeKok did not answer. It was one of his annoying habits. He could suddenly ignore everything and everybody around him, as if nothing else existed. Vledder knew the habit and had long since learned to live with it. Something seemed to amuse DeKok. A mischievous smile played around his lips.

He suddenly halted in front of an impressive canal house and pointed toward a brass plate, set in the dark stone of the facade. The brass plate was highly polished and gleamed in the rays of the Spring sun.

"*Dr. Charles P. Beaumonde, M.D., PhD.*" read Vledder. He also read the next two lines: "*Psychiatrist - Consultations strictly by appointment only.*"

DeKok grinned.

"Well, what do you think? Are you in the mood for a consultation?" He winked at Vledder. "Surely there's a little psychiatric repression somewhere."

"The man is dead," growled Vledder, "He died more than five years ago."

"A natural death . . . I hope."

Vledder nodded.

"I checked, of course. Our records agree with those at Town Hall. He died of a heart attack and had no police record. Charles Paul Beaumonde was sixty-six years old. He was survived by a relatively young wife and a son from a previous marriage."

DeKok nodded approvingly.

"My compliments, you're well informed." He paused. "What does 'relatively young' mean?" he asked as an afterthought.

"She's now about thirty-seven."

"A difference of thirty-four years?"

Vledder nodded calmly.

"Don't look so shocked. It's not all that unusual, these days. Anyway, it's about the only sin we can place at his doorstep. If it is a sin. Not a hint of scandal, or any other kind of controversy, during his lifetime. On the contrary: Dr. Beaumonde was known as a man of integrity and completely trustworthy. He was also very much admired in professional circles. He published a number of articles and a few books. I think I remember the title of one book: *Therapeutic Indications in the Treatment of the Mentally Impaired*, or something very much like it. He was one of the foremost practitioners of hypnosis in psychiatric therapy."

DeKok raised his hands in defense.

"Please spare me the psychiatric jargon."

Vledder looked crestfallen.

"But I thought the hypnosis thing was especially interesting. It's a bit old-fashioned today. Apparently it's not used that often anymore," His eyes twinkled as he added. "I thought that the old-fashioned nature of his treatments would appeal to you."

DeKok did not react to the reference about his preference for old-fashioned times.

"Who says it's not used anymore, at least not often?"

"I just called a few psychiatrists until I found one who knew Beaumonde personally. He was delighted that anybody showed interest. As I said, Beaumonde had a certain fame, in his time."

DeKok rubbed the bridge of his nose with a little finger. Then he thought better of it and after some searching found a toffee in a breast pocket. He unwrapped it and put it in his mouth. Absentmindedly he put the wrapper back in his breast pocket.

"Did your informant have any theories about your interest?"

Vledder shook his head, grinning.

"Not entirely. I just told him I was a cop and was interested in psychiatry. I had just happened to come across an article by Beaumonde and didn't understand it. Could he help?"

"And he explained it to you, did he?"

"More or less."

DeKok placed a hand on Vledder's shoulder.

"I don't know where you get your ideas, my boy, but that was pretty sneaky."

Vledder laughed.

"I just took a leaf out of your book. Anyway, the psychiatrist was a pleasant man ... over the telephone. He did say that he could not rid himself of the impression that he, and his colleagues, were viewed with a certain amount of suspicion by the police in general."

"Well, that impression is correct," said DeKok. "Perhaps it's not justified. I've never yet seen anybody come out of prison completely rehabilitated. Perhaps psychiatric institutions offer a better alternative." He sucked contently on his toffee. "What about Beaumonde's first wife?" he asked business-like.

Vledder pulled out his notebook, glanced at it to refresh his memory and then put it back.

"She died quite suddenly ... hemorrhage of the brain. Several years after her death he married again, to Estella Breevoorde."

For a while longer they remained in front of the building, staring at the facade and then, turning and leaning against the railing of the steps that led to the front door, they surveyed the canal. DeKok thought about the many crimes that had been committed on, or near the ancient canal. Then he turned again and motioned for Vledder to follow him.

Slowly they climbed the bluestone steps to the small porch in front of the door.

"Estella," said DeKok thoughtfully. "A beautiful name." From the porch he looked at a sightseeing boat that passed by like a large, white swan. "Estella ..." he murmured, "... it means 'star' ... the star of Breevoorde." He pushed the doorbell. "It's about time we make her acquaintance."

11

The heavy front door opened partially.

"Who is there?" asked a trembling female voice.

DeKok wanted to push the door further, but noticed it was on a chain.

"My name is DeKok," he said in a friendly voice, "DeKok with kay-oh-kay. I'm a police Inspector attached to Warmoes Street station and I am accompanied by my colleague, Vledder. We'd like to talk to you."

Part of a face appeared in the narrow opening. The single eye that was visible showed uncertainty and fear.

"Police?"

DeKok took off his hat and smiled amiably. With his other hand he reached an inside pocket and then showed his identification.

The door closed and then opened wide. A beautiful, slender woman stood in the door opening. She had a finely chiseled, oval face. Her skin was pale, contrasting with the jet-black hair that was gathered in a pony-tail.

DeKok bowed with old-world charm.

"Estella Beaumonde?"

She nodded distantly and made an inviting gesture.

DeKok came closer and noticed with surprise that the fear had left her eyes and the uncertainty had almost completely disappeared. She closed the door behind them and then led the way through a wide, marble corridor with intricate stucco work on the ceiling. Halfway down the corridor she opened the door to a spacious room with an exquisite selection of old paintings on the walls.

* * *

After the Inspectors had seated themselves, she took a chair across from them. With an easy, elegant movement she crossed her legs. Her back was straight and she folded her hands in her lap. There was something in her attitude and posture that forced respect; a pose of untouchable authority.

She observed the two men with her dark-brown eyes. Again DeKok was struck by the distance in her look. She looked at her visitors as if they were specimen on a laboratory slide.

"To what do I owe the pleasure of this visit?" she asked. Her voice was chilly and disdainful.

DeKok leaned forward.

"We," he said, "are in charge of an investigation relating to two murders."

"And for that you come here?"

DeKok took his hat from his knees and placed it on the floor.

"Yes, the curious fact is, that both men, the victims, had your husband's phone number in their pocket agendas." He smiled apologetically. "It's entirely possible that you can give us a plausible reason for that."

"Who are these men?" she asked, tilting her head back, as if to put more distance between her and the cops.

"Jan-Willem Hoffman and Alexander Peetersen."

She answered almost at once.

"Both were my husband's patients."

"You *recognize* the names?"

"No question about it," she said with conviction. "I know all the names of my husband's patients."

"Your husband . . . eh, died about five years ago. As far as we know, nobody else took over the practice."

"That is correct."

DeKok glanced at Vledder who was bent over his notebook.

"Why," asked DeKok, "should previous patients of your husband still have his phone number in their agendas?"

"Old notebooks?"

"Brand new . . . this year's."

"That is strange. Indeed."

DeKok cocked his head at her.

"You . . . eh, you don't maintain any contact with your husband's patients?"

She looked surprised.

"No . . . why should I?"

"Not even with the men I just named?"

She shrugged her shoulders with irritation.

"No . . . I just know their names from the patient files. The files were my responsibility and I kept them updated. It was part of my duties to make the bills up at the end of each quarter. I did that with the aid of the cards my husband used for his notes. I never had any personal contact with the patients. I don't think my husband would have liked that."

DeKok nodded understandingly.

"You live here alone?"

She did not answer at once. For the first time there was a certain hesitation.

"Sometimes I have guests . . . visitors."

"Family?"

She looked him full in the face. Her dark-brown eyes sparkled and her lips parted slightly.

"Not always . . . family."

DeKok hid a smile behind his hand. Her understatement had not escaped him.

"You only live here?"

She shook her head. The black hair swung from one shoulder to the other.

"No other residences, if that's what you mean. Of course, I'm not here all the time either. I spend the weekends with my parents in Bloemendaal and I make several vacation trips per year, from a few days to a few weeks."

DeKok paused, gathered his thoughts. He moved uneasily in his chair. There was something wrong about the interview. Estella Beaumonde responded too readily, too glibly, as if she had learned a lesson and now delivered it on cue. The picture she represented of herself was almost perfect. Perhaps a little naughty, but otherwise the spotless widow of a late, perfect psychiatrist. It was too smooth, too uncomplicated. He sighed deeply.

"The patient's cards . . . you still have them?"

Her eyes brightened.

"Certainly. They are complete. After my husband's passing, I prepared the final bills. The box with the cards is still in his study." She unfolded her hands and pointed toward the ceiling. "Just above here. I have left the room in its original condition. I mean, since my husband passed away, I haven't changed a thing. Everything is still in its place, the way my husband left it. The room is cleaned regularly, of course, dusted and so on . . . as if Charles were still alive. I've only changed the former waiting room, at the front of the house. I've started to use it." The corners of her mouth moved, it was not quite a smile.

"There were no memories attached to the waiting room," she added.

DeKok pressed his lips together. Again he had the feeling he was listening to a well-memorized, rehearsed speech. It was impersonal, like the voice on an answering machine. He forced a smile.

"May I see your husband's study?" he asked casually.

She nodded and stood up.

"Shall I lead the way?"

She preceded them out of the door, back to the marble corridor and then to an elaborate staircase with hand-carved wooden railings. She stopped at the bottom of the stairs and allowed the men to pass her.

She left little room and DeKok passed so closely that his arm brushed briefly against her breast. Immediately he noticed how she pressed closer. Suddenly he knew what bothered him. Her undeniable beauty lacked something essential. It lacked human warmth, the sparkling charm of a personality. She was like an artificial flower, ingenuous, beautiful, but sterile.

The study of the late Charles Paul Beaumonde was old-fashioned, but stylishly furnished. There was a roll-top desk and a wide, leather couch. Four oak-and-leather easy chairs were grouped around a low table. An exquisite Persian carpet covered the polished, wooden floor. In the corner, next to a window, was a safe. DeKok squatted down in front of the safe. He had seldom seen such an old safe. The green lacquer had peeled in several places and rusty metal was visible in the bare spots.

Estella came to stand next to him.

"The box of Pandora," she said.

DeKok looked up at her, a question on his face.

"Pandora's box?" he asked.

She nodded slowly.

"Pandora's box . . . that's what Charles called his safe. I was never allowed to look inside. That box, he would say, is full of disasters, catastrophes and other bad business. It's better to keep it closed."

DeKok rose from his squatting position.

"And you did?"

She looked at him evenly. Her face was paler.

"I never opened that safe. Not even after my husband's death. I don't even know what happened to the key."

"Aren't you curious?"

"No."

"Unfeminine."

She stared at him briefly.

"Maybe you're right . . . the suppression of curiosity may be an unfeminine characteristic. It's a point of view. In any case, I didn't want to repeat Pandora's mistake."

DeKok shrugged.

"An old Greek myth," he said carelessly.

Estella Beaumonde shook her head vehemently. Her dark eyes glowed in a chalk-white face.

"Not a myth," she panted, "No myth!" Trembling, she pointed at the old safe. "It is indeed filled with disasters, catastrophes and evil. They seem to ooze out, even without opening the door."

Suddenly she went to the roll-top desk. Near the bottom, on the right, she opened a drawer. She returned hastily with a letter in her hand.

"Perhaps . . . perhaps I would never have contacted the police . . . but . . . since you are here . . ."

She did not complete the sentence, but visibly affected, she handed the letter to DeKok.

DeKok turned the letter over in his hand several times. The addressing was correct, in large, shaky block letters. The name

116

"Beaumonde" had been spelled correctly. The envelope was recently post-marked in Hoorn, a small town on the coast of the former Zuyder Zee. There was no name of a sender. He sniffed the envelope and noticed a hint of lavender.

"When did you receive this letter?"

"This morning."

"You opened it?"

"Yes."

DeKok opened the envelope, took the letter out and unfolded it. A sentence had been pasted in the middle of the sheet. The message had been compiled from roughly cut-out letters out of a newspaper. With a shock he glanced at her. Vledder read over his shoulder.

"FLEE," he read, "IF YOU LOVE LIFE!"

* * *

From Emperors Canal they crossed Lily Canal toward Tower Gates and from there toward Mole Alley until they reached Count Street. DeKok remained silent as they walked along. In his mind he replayed the entire conversation with Estella Beaumonde. He again reviewed every word, every gesture, every expression of her dark-brown eyes. It was an ability that had grown on him and had been perfected over the many years of his career. Vledder often said that sometimes DeKok was better than a tape-recorder. Again DeKok reviewed her expressions, the look in her eyes. Thoughts, he knew, were not always expressed in words. The real thoughts were so often hidden behind a facade of meaningless sounds.

Vledder snorted.

"Flee, if you love life!" He shook his head. "I can't believe it. It's too old-fashioned, too melodramatic . . . it's got to be a

117

joke." he looked a question at DeKok. "Are you taking it seriously?"

DeKok pushed back his little hat and scratched the top of his head.

"It *did* affect her."

Vledder grinned.

"At first I thought she had ice-water in her veins. What a cool customer. That old psychiatrist can't have had much fun with her."

DeKok gave him a stern look.

"I hope you're not developing into one of these people that always have to talk about sex. But," he continued in a lecturing tone of voice, "you may be mistaken. Such seemingly cool women may be very passionate in their love life. I have that from some authorities in the field."

"Your friends in the Quarter?"

DeKok did not deign to answer the allusion to his contacts in the Red Light District. Instead he continued a different train of thought.

"At first," he said pensively, "when she first opened the door, there was fear, uncertainty and precaution. That seemed to disappear quickly. But when she showed us the letter, she was clearly in the grip of strong emotions."

Vledder was perplexed.

"You . . . you *are* taking the letter seriously!?"

DeKok raised a finger in the air.

"*She* takes it seriously."

Vledder shook his head.

"You mean," he began hesitantly, "you mean . . . that she . . . may have good reasons to take that letter seriously? That she does *not* consider it a joke?"

DeKok grinned broadly.

"These rare moments of insight, Dick . . . I admire that."

"Go fly a kite."

Vledder was still peeved and grumpy as he preceded a laughing DeKok into the station. Meindert Post, with a face like a thundercloud, leaned on the railing. As soon as he saw DeKok, he roared out.

"Man . . . where *have* you been? You're always out! Never there when you're wanted. Everybody has been looking for you."

DeKok looked at the bulky Watch Commander.

"What's up?" he asked mildly.

Meindert was not yet ready to tell him.

"Why don't you carry a walkie-talkie?" he demanded. "Or at least, let Vledder use one. This is the 20th Century, man. No reason to be out of touch."

"Perhaps that's what is wrong with the Century," answered DeKok. "Now will you tell me what's the matter?"

"They fished a man out of the Old Waal."

"And?"

"They said you're looking for him."

It took DeKok a few moments before the words penetrated. Then he covered his eyes with his hands and looked at Post through spread fingers.

"Red Bakker?"

Meindert Post nodded.

12

DeKok jumped from the quay onto the foredeck of the old houseboat. He walked along the narrow gangway to the stern. Vledder was close behind. On the stern deck they found the corpse of a man. Dirty river water dripped from his clothes and shaped bizarre rivulets of water that drained away through the scuppers. Next to the corpse were two morgue attendants, the stretcher vertically between them. A young constable approached DeKok.

"The resident of this houseboat saw him floating by. I called the Drown-Unit, who fished him out of the water. When they saw they could do nothing with him, they alerted the morgue. There was a lot of rubbernecking and a man in the crowd yelled that Inspector DeKok was looking for this man."

"What sort of man?'

"The one who yelled?"

"Yes."

The constable shrugged his shoulders.

"I forgot to get his name, what with the crowd and all. Anyway, he didn't hang around and left almost immediately."

"What did he look like?"

"A small man with a mousey face."

DeKok smiled.

"I'll find him."

He crouched down next to the corpse. It was Red Bakker, without a doubt. He was easily recognizable. The immersion in the water had hardly damaged his face. DeKok unbuttoned the overcoat of the dead man. Then he opened the jacket underneath and pulled up on the lapels. Beneath the jacket, on the white shirt, he found three bullet holes, close together.

Vledder squatted next to his old partner.

"Damn," said the young man, "just like the others."

DeKok nodded slowly. A tired feeling of helplessness came over him. How many more times would the murderer strike? How many more corpses would he have to view until he found the killer? Slowly he came to a standing position, his knees creaked with the effort.

"Has the Coroner been yet?"

The young constable nodded and consulted his notebook.

"A strange old man. At first I thought he was dressed up for a fancy ball, or a stage play. His name is Dr. Koning. He said the man was dead."

"Thanks," grinned DeKok. He motioned toward the morgue attendants. "Take him directly to the police lab."

The men nodded in unison, placed the stretcher next to the corpse and unrolled the body bag. Before long, Red Bakker's earthly remains were encased in the bag and the bag was securely attached to the stretcher. Without any apparent discomfort from the motion of the houseboat, the morgue attendants disappeared with their burden. A heave and a push and the stretcher was on the quay.

DeKok watched as they shoved the stretcher into the car and drove off. Red Bakker was a rat. One of the many rats in Amsterdam's crime jungle. He sighed and rubbed his face with his hands. Yet, he thought, I wouldn't have wished a death like that on anyone, even Red Bakker. With his head down, DeKok followed Vledder back to the side of the river. As Vledder leaned down to help him up the steep brick wall, DeKok muttered to himself. Sometimes he even cared about rats.

Vledder pointed at the morgue vehicle in the distance.

"Want me to follow them?"

"Yes," said DeKok. "As soon as they have stripped him, take the contents of his pockets. Look for an agenda and a street map of Amsterdam."

"Then what?"

"Take the stuff to the station and see if you can snare Fred Prins. Maybe you can enlist a few more detectives."

"What for?"

DeKok made a gesture indicating his surroundings.

"To search. I don't think that our killer is the type to keep dragging a corpse around for long. I don't think that happened. Red Bakker must have been killed close by and then tossed into the drink. I'm betting that the shells are somewhere around here. As soon as you've found them, do a house-to-house in the neighborhood. Ask if anybody has seen anything ... heard something."

Vledder nodded.

"What about you?"

"I'm going to see Lowee."

Vledder raised his watch demonstratively in front of DeKok's face.

"A bit early isn't it?"

DeKok looked at his partner for several seconds. There was a disappointed look on his face. Without a word he turned around and ambled away in his typical, somewhat waddling gait.

* * *

Little Lowee hastily dried his hands on the front of his shirt.

"I were just coming from me old Mom at Chalk Mart and I see 'em fishing the stiff from the Old Waal."

"And then you told the constable I was looking for him."

"Exactum." Little Lowee looked worried. "You is, ain't you?"

DeKok nodded encouragingly.

"I needed him as a witness in a murder case."

"And now he's peiger."*

"Murdered . . . three bullets in the chest."

The barkeeper snorted.

"They falls like dominos nowadays."

DeKok moved on his barstool.

"Don't you think it's strange?"

Little Lowee shook his head calmly, a knowing look on his face.

"Red Bakker made a lotta enemies in his life . . . a small army, iffen you ax me. He *breeded* them, you knows. Tha' was his main job. He done give a lotta people nasty times. You just cain't do that without somebody hittin' back. There's always one that don't take it no more, you knows."

DeKok stared into the distance.

"Didn't you say something about him making a big haul?"

Little Lowee nodded with conviction.

"Yessir, Black Judy done tole me. He done found a little gold-mine. The guy only had to fork over, was all, cross over the bridge, you knows."

DeKok nodded thoughtfully.

"Maybe that's exactly what he did . . . cross the bridge, the bridge across the Old Waal . . . with a pistol in his hand." He

---

*Peiger (pronounced pie-gur, with the "g" as the "ch" in Loch): Amsterdam slang for *deceased*.

chewed his lower lip. "Is Black Judy still in Old Acquaintance Alley?"

Lowee pointed toward the opposite wall.

"Yep, right next to Flemish Gilda. Upstairs. You gotta take the blue steps witta green door. She be home now, I's sure."

"Does she know?"

Lowee shrugged.

"Mebbe . . . mebbe they done tole 'er."

DeKok slid off the stool.

"How deep was the love between those two?"

Little Lowee looked depressed.,

"Whadda you cal 'luv' with them guys?"

* * *

DeKok hoisted his two hundred pounds up the narrow, rickety stairs. The moldy threads creaked under his weight. He did not bother to knock but just entered the small room.

Black Judy, dressed in a robe, was seated in front of a small electric heater. She did not seem concerned about his unannounced visit. She looked at DeKok with a wide smile on her face.

"Are you here as the heat, or as a john?"

DeKok took a chair next to her.

"I better not leave the choice to you."

She pressed her breasts together and out and gave him an enticing look.

"You don't know what you're missing."

DeKok remained serious.

"I know what you're missing," he said carefully while looking into her face.

Her expression changed. The seriousness on the face of the Inspector confused her.

"What are you talking about?"

DeKok swallowed, always nervous at moments like this.

"What you're missing . . . if I told you that we just fished Red Bakker out of the water?"

Her eyes opened wide.

"Is . . . is he dead?"

DeKok nodded.

"Murdered."

She leaned back in her chair. Her face, under the excessive makeup, paled.

"I was afraid of that," she whispered. "I thought it would happen, sooner or later . . . sooner or later."

"What?" interrupted DeKok.

"That they would kill him."

"Who?"

She spread her arms, causing the robe to fall open to reveal her superb figure.

"You know how Red Bakker made his money," she said, absent-mindedly closing the robe. "He lived off dirty money. *Mister Cunning Cheat*, they called him. He was a rat, just a rat. No more. He even cheated me. Money that belonged to my mother and . . ."

DeKok interrupted again.

"Wasn't he about to make a big haul."

She leaned forward and sideways, placing a confidential hand on DeKok's knee in an animated gesture. Her face regained some of its color and made the make-up stand out to its best advantage. She was very desirable this way and it looked as if she had already overcome her grief. She shook her head.

"Ach," she said, "I've known Red for so long. Before now I used to run around with him in the past as well, a few years at least. Bakker always had tall tales, big plans about enormous hauls . . . about little gold mines . . . about guys, flush with money ... and he knew something about them that they wouldn't like to be known. You understand, he lived in phantasies, *on* phantasies." She paused and sat up straighter. "I'd be lying if I said he treated me bad. Not that. He always made something ... but it was never something that would make him big. Small, nasty jobs, you know what I mean?"

DeKok's gaze travelled through the little room. On the small dresser was a picture of Red Bakker in better days.

"I'm looking for his killer, Judy," he said calmly. "I'm looking for the person who put three bullets in his chest. And I need your help. It's not at all unlikely that the big haul he talked about, dreamed about, had something to do with his death."

She nodded slowly.

"That's possible."

DeKok pushed his chair a little closer.

"What did he tell you?"

She brought her hand to her mouth and suddenly there were tears. They dripped from her black-outlined eyes and fell on the shiny material of the robe.

"Poor Red ... you know, DeKok ... he was so sure this time ... so sure. There was no way it could go wrong."

"What?"

Black Judy controlled herself with an effort. She pulled a lace handkerchief from a pocket and blotted her eyes.

"That guy had said that he would very much like to have the pictures and they were worth a bundle to him."

"What kind of pictures?"

She sighed.

"Pictures of a guy in women's clothing. Red Bakker had taken them himself, on the sly. The guy never knew. Then Red offered them for sale."

"For how much?"

"A hundred thousand."

"That much?"

"That's what the guy was willing to pay."

DeKok whistled between his teeth.

"A lot of money for some pictures."

She grimaced.

"Perhaps that guy didn't want anyone to know that he dressed up in women's clothes."

DeKok made a nonchalant gesture.

"But who cares about that? Especially in Amsterdam. There are so many transvestites."

She snorted and wrinkled her nose.

"If they dare admit it, there's no problem. Red was surprised too, that the guy was willing to pay that much."

DeKok looked at her sharply.

"Who *is* the guy."

She spread her arms again, in a gesture of surrender. Again she revealed her superb figure. DeKok never took his eyes off her face. She closed the robe and shrugged.

"If I knew, DeKok, believe me, I'd tell you. Really. Whenever Red talked about him, he always referred to 'that guy' and he never gave any indication who it was. He never mentioned a name. Red Bakker could be very secretive."

"Did you see the photo's?"

She shook her head sadly.

"Red probably has them stashed in a bank safety deposit box, complete with negatives. That's the way he did things. He *never* had anything in the house."

There was something in Judy's story that was unbelievable, thought DeKok. There was something unreal about it, strange, bizarre. It set him to thinking.

"When were the pictures made?"

"Recently."

DeKok pushed his lower lip forward and rubbed the bridge of his nose with a little finger. Then he leaned closer to her.

"Why," he asked sharply, "why did Red make pictures of *this* guy and not of other transvestites? Also . . . how did he know the guy was a transvestite?"

She leaned back, away from his stern eyes. The questions confused her.

"That . . . eh, I don't know that," she stammered. "Red Bakker had met an old mate, a gigolo, you know what I mean? A guy that goes to bed with older women, for money." She wrinkled her nose as if male prostitution was something reprehensible, compared to her own, honest profession. "Anyway, that's who told him."

DeKok was getting impatient.

"Who told him? Who was this mate?"

She started to cry, bowed her head and hid her face in her hands.

"You'll have to ask Red . . . you'll have to ask Red."

DeKok stood up. He placed a comforting hand on her shaking shoulders and squeezed lightly. Then he left the room and descended the stairs.

Outside he took a deep breath. Even the air in Old Acquaintance Alley seemed preferable to the atmosphere in the sad little room.

13

Vledder pointed at the table on which he had displayed the personal possessions of Red Bakker. The nice clothes of the late blackmailer had been shoved into a plastic bag and placed under the table. The shirt with the three bullet holes on top.

"That's all of it."

"Anything special?"

Vledder nodded and picked a wet pocket agenda from the table. He showed it to DeKok and pointed.

"Look, the phone number of that psychiatrist at Emperors Canal, the dead one. Just like the others. It's just been written in at a later date. The handwriting is a bit different. I think when Red started using the agenda at the beginning of the year, he didn't know the number yet. It's written apart from the other numbers and with a different pen." He looked at DeKok. "We could ask Estella Beaumonde if Red Bakker was also one of her husband's patients."

DeKok looked at the large clock against the wall.

"It's almost ten o'clock."

"So?"

"She probably won't be home. She visits her parents on the weekends." DeKok shrugged his shoulders. "It's not that urgent." He brought the conversation back to the agenda. "Anything else that you found remarkable?"

Vledder shook his head.

"Not in the agenda. It's almost impossible to make sense out of those scribbles. Apart for the phone numbers, he might as well have been writing in Sanskrit."

DeKok grinned.

"Apparently he had a lot to hide during his lifetime." He surveyed the items on the table. "Was there a map for Amsterdam?"

"Yes, I was coming to that. A street map, complete with an X that marks the spot. That made it easy. Fred went to the place and found the expended shells."

"Where?"

"Near Montelbaan Tower on Old Bulwark. Just across from the Old Waal. We think that after the shooting the body was thrown into the waters of Old Bulwark Canal, near the Tower and then, during the sluicing of the canals, it drifted toward the Old Waal."

DeKok easily visualized Montelbaan Tower, considered to be the most perfectly proportioned tower in Amsterdam. It dominated an especially picturesque part of Amsterdam, which was very picturesque in its own right. The tower is only a stone's throw from the house where Rembrandt lived for almost twenty years. And it was a fact, he considered, that the waters in the Amsterdam canals were regularly replenished with fresh water from the Ijssel Lake. The "old" water was pumped out into the North Sea.

"Yes, it could have happened that way," said DeKok. He visualized the map of Amsterdam again. "As the crow flies," he continued, "Montelbaan Tower is close to Lastage Road where Peetersen was killed. The murderer seems to prefer that general area."

Vledder did not agree.

"But Rembrandt Park is in the Sixth District," remarked Vledder. "It's a bit out of the way." He raked his fingers through his hair.

"Jan-Willem Hoffman, Alexander Peetersen, Red Bakker ... three killings ... the same murderer ... we're not even close."

Vledder was distracted by the movement of the door to the busy detective room. Idly he watched as a young man entered. The man was short, slender and with an honest, open face. DeKok followed Vledder's gaze and saw the young man approach the desk nearest the door. The detective at the desk looked up from his keyboard and listened to the shy question. Then he pointed across the room in the direction of Vledder and DeKok.

The visitor turned around and followed the direction of the pointed finger. DeKok estimated the visitor to be in his late twenties. The young man wore a brown, tweed jacket with patches on the elbows. Dark blond hair curled down to the collar of his checked shirt.

"Are you Inspector DeKok?"

The gray sleuth smiled pleasantly.

"Yes, I am. How can I help you?"

The young man swallowed, obviously he had some difficulty with how to proceed.

"My name is Felix," he said finally. "Yes, Felix Beaumonde. I would like to talk to you." He darted a quick glance in Vledder's direction. "Privately."

DeKok pointed at the chair next to his desk.

"Please have a seat and go ahead. Don't worry about my colleague ... discretion is his middle name ... that's why we recruited him."

Felix Beaumonde pulled up on the legs of his spotless trousers and sat down at the edge of the chair. He did not react to DeKok's jocular tone.

"It's about my mother . . . or rather, my stepmother . . . yes, Estella Beaumonde."

DeKok nodded.

"We visited her this morning."

The young man worried with his tie.

"Yes, I heard about that, yes. She . . . eh, she received a threatening letter."

"That's a bit strong, surely," objected DeKok.

"Not a threatening letter?"

DeKok shook his head.

"No, not in that sense. It's more a warning."

"A warning of what"

DeKok looked at him evenly.

"Approaching danger."

Felix made tut-tut sounds and shook his head sadly.

"Yes, well, it's hard to have to say this, Inspector, yes. But it's her own fault."

DeKok's eyebrows suddenly came to life. Felix's mouth opened wide, then he blinked his eyes rapidly several time and shook his head as if to clear his vision. Vledder grinned to himself. He had missed the unusual movements of DeKok's eyebrows, but he was certain from the young man's reaction that they had behaved in top form. DeKok's eyebrows simply did not seem to fit in with the normal aspects of human anatomy. Not for the first time, Vledder thought about the antennae of an insect.

DeKok waited patiently while Felix recovered from his momentary confusion. He seemed unaware of his eyebrows and the effect they had on people.

"Her own fault?" prompted DeKok.

"Yes," answered Beaumonde, still not sure about what he had seen, "yes, her own fault. She's always associating with . . . yes, with suave . . . eh, persons."

"Suave . . . how?"

"Yes, well, shortly after my father died, Estella started to do strange things, yes. She seemed abandoned, wild, yes? Clearly she was on the road to ruin. Yes, instead of looking for a decent, respectable gentleman for a second marriage, she . . . yes, she sought the company of young men . . . yes, who she *paid* for their services."

"Gigolos?"

The young man rubbed his cheek with the tips of his fingers.

"Yes, I . . . eh, yes, I believe that is what they are called. Yes, I have often found her in the company of such men. Sometimes I said something about it . . . yes, a warning, so to speak. But she seemed to be too . . . yes, too insensitive, or maybe too involved to notice."

DeKok leaned closer.

"Your stepmother is still a very attractive woman," he said in a conspiratorial tone of voice. "She seems extremely charming. Surely she is allowed to meet men in the usual way."

Beaumonde turned his head away.

"Yes, well, I never heard my father complain about it, but perhaps Estella is . . . yes, over-sexed . . . yes, perhaps her desires are more than . . . yes, perhaps she cannot be satisfied by a single man."

DeKok hid a smile at so much naivety.

"But that is still not a reason to *buy* love. I know several women who have sexual relationships with more than one man . . . and they feel just fine."

Felix wrung his hands.

"Yes, well, maybe. I just don't know what can be the matter. Yes, what bothers Estella? Yes, I would like to know . . . but as her, yes, as her stepson, I'm not in a position to question her behavior."

DeKok reacted surprised, a little annoyed.

"Buy why should you? I don't find her behavior, the way you describe it, at all exceptional, peculiar. Some people are addicted to alcohol. Others ruin themselves with drugs. When it comes to excesses . . . I think sex is preferable."

Felix Beaumonde shook his head stubbornly.

"Yes, but I worry."

"You're taking the warning seriously?"

"Yes, I am. Yes."

"And you suspect it comes from the circle of friends she has cultivated, lately?"

"Yes, certainly. Yes."

"Do you know any of the men?"

Beaumonde raised his hands in a gesture of despair.

"Yes, from time to time Estella has introduced me to some of them, yes. But I don't remember the names. They don't interest me. Yes, on the contrary, they seem abhorrent to me."

DeKok rubbed the bridge of his nose with a little finger. After a while he lowered his hand and looked at the finger as if he had never seen it before. Then he stretched out his arm toward Felix Beaumonde.

"The problem is," said DeKok, "how do you place such a warning in the context you describe? What is the reason? A quarrel, jealousy? You tell me."

"Yes, that I don't know. Maybe blackmail . . . yes, why not? I don't know the background. Estella doesn't discuss her private life with me. Yes, she keeps that closely hidden. I don't know how she got into difficulties . . . I don't."

"Is she?"

"What?"

"In difficulties?"

"Yes, oh, yes. She has received a second letter."

"When?"

"This afternoon, yes, this afternoon. It must have been pushed under the door. Yes, Estella called me about it before she left for Bloemendaal."

"Not by mail?"

"No . . . no, not by mail."

"And the text?"

Felix looked pale.

"FLEE . . . YOU'RE TOO YOUNG TO DIE!"

* * *

The words still seemed to echo from the walls, long after Felix Beaumonde had left.

Vledder looked at his partner.

"Yes," he grimaced, "and then there's that, yes?"

"Yes," said DeKok with a smile.

"Yes, well," said Vledder, "but seriously . . . Is Estella really in danger? How and why? I find it hard to believe. It looks more like a macabre joke."

DeKok growled.

"I can't see the joke."

"Well . . . for instance, those, how did he say it? Those *suave* guys, those gigolos, they're not usually violent, are they? Or do you know different?"

DeKok shook his head.

"If there *is* a danger for Estella, I don't think we have to look for it in *that* direction. As long as those boys are being paid for their . . . eh, their services, they'll keep coming back. If she stops paying, they simply stay away. Unless, of course, one of them decides to continue the relationship *per amore*, for love, that is." He paused and stared into the distance. "There are some cases of blackmail by a gigolo, but I just can't see Estella as the victim of blackmail. She's a liberated woman, without moral obligations. And, listening to Felix, Estella knows exactly what she wants and knows exactly how to go about getting it."

Vledder was just about to answer, when he stopped, his mouth half open. Quickly he recovered from his surprise. Little Lowee had appeared in the door opening.

Disdaining directions from anybody, Lowee confidently found his way to DeKok's desk. DeKok stood up from behind his desk and met him half-way.

"Did you close your establishment?" asked DeKok.

Lowee shook his head. Now that he had found DeKok he seemed to have lost some of his self-confidence. DeKok understood. The small barkeeper did not like to be seen at the station. There was always the possibility somebody would suspect him of being an informer. An unhealthy occupation in any criminal society.

"Karl is keepin' it covered," said Lowee.

"Let's go in here," said DeKok and opened a door to one of the small interrogation rooms. Lowee gave him a grateful look as he darted inside. Vledder closed the door after all three had entered and while Lowee and DeKok sat down at the table, Vledder leaned against the door.

"I dinna wanna wait," said Lowee. "It were scratching me gut, you knows. So I just sorta rushed over, quick like. Downstairs they done tole me you was here still."

DeKok gave him a searching look.

"What's up, Lowee?"

The small barkeeper sighed.

"I dunno, don't wanna have nuthin' to do with it. Tha's why I come, you knows? In case the sh . . . , eh, somewhat happen."

"What happens?"

Lowee was clearly ill at ease.

"I hadda coupla broads inna bar ... working girls, you knows ... anna some wise guys. They done seen the guy and they hear what he says."

"What sort of guy?"

"That guy, that wanna buy some heaters."

"Pistols?"

"Pistols, heaters, who cares. He was lookin' for eleven."

DeKok stared at his small friend.

"Eleven?"

Lowee spread wide his arms.

"Itsa crazy, I knows. I dinna wanna talk about it."

DeKok leaned closer.

"Explain."

"Well, you knows, this guy, he says where can I buy some heaters, and I says heaters, what do you mean? And he says, you knows where I can buy some and I says no."

"You didn't send him to Blue Max? Or Pistol Pete?"

"No way. You gotta believe me, DeKok. I don't mind makin' an extra buck now and then, but heaters ... come on, I don't wanna have nuthin' to do with that."

"Did he get the weapons?"

The small barkeeper did not answer. He moved restlessly in his chair and evaded DeKok's eyes. DeKok leaned closer still.

"Did he get them?" he repeated.

Little Lowee sighed a deep sigh.

"I dunno. Really. But I thinks he do. You see, that guy had lotsa moolah and then ..."

DeKok interrupted.

"What sort of guy? How old?"

"About fifty. Mebbe older. Tall, skinny sorta geezer. Talkin' pretty toff, you knows, like he don't knows you're human too . . . nice threads."

DeKok slapped his hand on the table.

"The tall, skinny man," he said tonelessly. For several seconds he stared at his visitor, then he jumped up, knocking over his chair. He gestured toward Lowee. "Back to the bar," he ordered, "and try to find out if the guy made the purchase and if so, who from."

Lowee looked anxious.

"Think of me reputacy," he protested.

DeKok smiled suddenly.

"Of course, your reputation. I understand. Never mind, I'd be the last person in the world to cause you trouble."

Lowee gave him a suspicious look, but left gratefully as soon as Vledder held open the door.

DeKok turned to Vledder.

"Get a hold of Mrs. Breevoorde, use the telephone."

Despite everything, Vledder laughed inwardly. Only DeKok would find it necessary to clarify the use of a telephone.

"Who is that?" asked Vledder.

DeKok shook his head, a sad look on his face.

"How soon we forget. She's the mother of Estella, in Bloemendaal. I want to know if everything is all right."

Vledder found a phone book and DeKok started pacing up and down. It was getting late and there seemed to be a lull in the traffic in and out of the detective room. There were only two other detectives still at their desk. Soon, DeKok knew, the procession would start again. Fights in bars, fights with prostitutes, fights among prostitutes, burglaries, robberies and the occasional murder. Warmoes Street station never closed. Meanwhile, with another part of his mind, he thought about the case. Somewhere there was a connection, somehow everything fit together . . . like a jig-saw puzzle. He paced on . . . ten feet one way, avoid a chair, another five feet, five feet back, avoid the same chair, another ten feet, turn, do it again. The world around him became less real, seemed to disappear. Until Vledder tapped him on the shoulder.

"No answer."

DeKok's face fell.

"Call the Bloemendaal police and ask then to check on the house. Maybe there's something wrong with the phone."

Vledder, who had his computer screen lit up, glanced at it and dialed a number. Within seconds he was talking to the Bloemendaal police. DeKok had resumed his pacing, but suddenly he stopped and turned toward Vledder. Something in the young man's voice had alerted him.

"What's going on?"

Vledder covered the mouthpiece with his hand.

"Bloemendaal wants to know why we're interested."

"Just tell them that we fear . . . fear an accident."

DeKok watched as Vledder passed on the message, Then Vledder paled.

"What's the matter?" asked DeKok.

Vledder replaced the receiver.

"They found Estella. An anonymous call. About half an hour ago."

"Where?"

"In the dunes, along the coast."

"And?"

"Murdered."

14

The clock in Warmoes Street station pointed to eleven thirty. DeKok still felt the shock of hearing the news of Estella's death. Vledder sat behind his desk and for once was not busy with his computer. DeKok wondered if he should have taken more seriously the warnings that Estella had received. Perhaps he should have informed the Bloemendaal police sooner.

Then he shrugged. That would have done little good. What could the local cops have done? There were no grounds to give her twenty-four hour protection, no real proof for the necessity. Besides, he thought, the total police force in Bloemendaal was probably less than a dozen men and women. They would simply have been unable to supply the personnel. And on what basis, anyway? He kept returning to that thought. A warning . . . who from . . . why?

With a conscious effort he cleared his mind and walked over to Vledder's desk.

"Go to Bloemendaal. Talk to whoever is handling the case and make a note of all the circumstances. Tell them about the warnings she received, but don't say a thing about our investigations. Nothing about Jan-Willem, Peetersen, or Red Bakker."

Vledder had reservations.

"Then how do I explain our visit to her, this morning?"

"Just tell them that she called us about the first letter she received and that we listened politely, but did not take the threat seriously. Perhaps they'll understand." He rubbed the back of his neck. "Just make sure they won't come to Amsterdam tonight, to search her house."

"And how," asked Vledder, "do you expect me to do that?"

"I don't care," answered DeKok, irritated. "Think of something . . . for all I care you let the air out of their tires."

Vledder gave him a suspicious look.

"And what about you?"

DeKok grabbed for his coat.

"Me? I'm going to see Handy Henkie. I think I'll need his expertise."

* * *

The ex-burglar gave DeKok a calculating look.

"I didn't throw them away, if that's what you mean."

DeKok grinned.

"That's exactly what I mean. If you still have your tools, I want you to take them out of mothballs."

"What for?"

"To open a safe."

"What kind of safe?"

DeKok unwrapped a stick of chewing gum and placed it behind his teeth. He chewed several times before answering.

"An old safe. From the beginning of this Century. A well-preserved example of the safe-makers craft. Easy as pie, for you." He rummaged in his pockets and showed a small brass tube. The tube contained an ingenious collection of parts. A long time ago, when Henkie had decided to go straight, he had given it to the cop as a sort of "going away present." Since that time, no lock had lasted long before it had yielded to Henkie's invention. DeKok held up the small instrument. "This little thing has helped me a lot, Henkie. It has helped a few times to discover the truth and I'll always be grateful to you. But I can't open that safe with it. I wouldn't even know where to start."

"What's in it?"

DeKok shook his head.

"Nothing . . . nothing for you."

"And for you?"

"I don't know," admitted DeKok. "Not exactly. But I have a vague idea, a hunch. No more."

Henkie pursed his lips and shook his head judiciously.

"I'd rather not, DeKok. I left all that behind, you know."

DeKok looked at him evenly.

"It may have a connection with the murder of Jan-Willem," he explained patiently. He came closer. "It would be nice for Josephine, wouldn't it, if it helps me to find the real killer?"

Henkie looked angry.

"They should never have arrested her. Josephine is innocent. And that's the truth."

DeKok smiled thinly.

"If you can't prove it, the truth can mean little these days. You have to have proof, Henkie. And as long as the real killer of Jan-Willem isn't caught, there will always be people who'll point the finger at Josephine. People don't forget. Believe me. Even your grandchildren will still suffer." He paused, hoping that he had been persuasive enough. "You simply can't refuse, Henkie. You've *got* to help me."

The old burglar scratched behind his ear, a thoughtful look on his face.

"What's the risk?"

"Hardly any."

"A safe, eh?"

"As I said . . . a piece of cake . . . for you."

* * *

It was quiet on Emperors Canal. They heard the footsteps of a late stroller from the direction of Lily Canal, the rustling of the trees and the occasional squawk of a stray rat. DeKok looked up at the illuminated face of the Wester Tower and saw it was almost two in the morning.

Henkie stood in front of the door, his raincoat like a cape around him. He did something incomprehensible and hissed at DeKok. The door was open. As DeKok climbed the few steps to the front door, Henkie entered the house. As soon as DeKok had joined him, the burglar closed the door softly.

Carefully they slunk along the wide, marble corridor. The light from their flashlights created strange shadows on the stucco ceiling. They reached the bottom of the finely carved stairway. Stepping near the sides of the treads, they climbed the stairs.

The late psychiatrist's office was not locked. They entered the room. Henkie immediately squatted down in front of the safe. With a happy gleam in his eyes, he looked at DeKok.

"What a sweetheart," he whispered happily. "What a nice little box. I didn't know they were still around. It is a museum piece, you know that? A safe like this is a beautiful piece of work."

DeKok grinned at the enthusiasm.

"Don't go all lyrical on me. Just open it, will you?"

Henkie looked at the serial number of the safe and then selected a tool from his tool belt.

DeKok watched for a little while. Then he went to the roll-top desk and sat on the chair in front of it. He took the cards for Jan-Willem Hoffman and Alex Peetersen from the box and looked at them carefully. In the upper right hand corner were numbers and various markings in different colors.

DeKok felt a glow inside. It was almost a physical thing and suddenly he *knew* with a calm certainty that in this room he would find the key to the murders. He rubbed the inside of his collar and looked at Henkie, who suddenly gave a suppressed exclamation of triumph.

"It's open."

DeKok left the desk. It was a solemn moment when Henkie moved the last few bolts and pulled open the heavy door of the safe. By the light of two flashlights they saw a number of racks, containing hundreds of small cassette tapes. Henkie looked at DeKok, a question in his eyes.

"This it?" There was disappointment and doubt in his voice.

DeKok licked suddenly dry lips.

"Let's take all the racks out. Let's put them on the couch, over there. That will be best. I want to know if any are missing. Then we can put them back."

Henkie nodded agreement.

"That should be easy to spot."

Steadily they worked, rack after rack, holder after holder, carrel after carrel. DeKok made careful notes.

They were almost finished when they suddenly heard footsteps outside the door. Somebody was climbing the stairs. Quickly they extinguished their flashlights.

The footsteps passed their door and climbed the next set of stairs to the floor above. There was nothing secretive in the steps. It sounded normal, the steps of somebody on familiar ground, somebody who belonged.

DeKok felt Henkie's breath on his neck.

"Who's that?" whispered the ex-burglar.

"I don't know. I had no idea that anybody was supposed to be coming here."

Handy Henkie growled.

"Some burglar, you are. You should have cased the joint."

DeKok snorted.

"If you'd never made mistakes in the past, I would never have caught you. Go ahead and close the safe the way you found it and take off."

"What about you?"

"I want to know who belongs to those footsteps."

"You want me to warn anybody?" Henkie sounded worried.

DeKok shook his head in the dark. Then, realizing Henkie could not see him, he spoke.

"You're a great guy, Henkie. I mean it. As soon as I have some time, I'll come and thank you in more detail. Now it's better if you don't run any more risks. It would be difficult to explain your presence here. Therefore it's better if you take off . . . for me, too." He grinned softly. "My regards to your family. Be careful and make sure I can get out, downstairs."

Handy Henkie turned toward the safe and had it closed and locked within seconds. Nobody would be able to tell that the safe had been opened illegally. Henkie tapped DeKok on the shoulder by way of greeting and disappeared in the darkness.

DeKok listened intently to the sounds of the house. Only after he heard Henkie's footsteps on the canal quay, did he open the door of the office and step into the corridor. To the right was a staircase leading up. Carefully he climbed the steps. There was nothing to be seen on the next floor. Then he discovered a staircase at the end that led up to yet another floor. For some reason the stairs in this old house had not been built on top of each other. He wondered about that, but then realized that the stairs all ran from front to back. Of course, he thought, in the old days Amsterdam houses were taxed depending on the amount of frontage they had. Therefore the houses of that period tended to be narrow, but deep.

When he arrived on the fourth floor, he noticed a light from under the door of a room. Softly he crept closer. He took the old-fashioned, wooden doorknob in one hand and turned it slowly. Then, with a sudden kick he threw the door wide open and with a yell he stormed into the room, the flashlight in one hand like a club.

It was a small room and next to the single bed stood a pale young man in striped pajamas. His mouth was half open and there was a look of fear and bewilderment in his eyes.

DeKok made the flashlight disappear in one of his pockets and grabbed the young man by the front of his pajamas. The thin material tore as he pulled the occupant of the room closer.

"Who are you?"

The young man, balancing on his toes in DeKok's iron grip, swallowed. His body shook with fear and there was a pinched look on his face.

"Robby . . . Robby Vanderwal."

15

DeKok looked at Vledder with a twinkling in his eyes. His young partner was sprawled behind his desk. His eyes were red and there was a wan, tired look in them.

"Tell me about it," said DeKok.

Vledder yawned.

"Those cops in Bloemendaal don't know when to quit. They seemed possessed with the case. I didn't get back home until four in the morning. And only because I insisted I was exhausted, because otherwise they would have followed me to Amsterdam to start a search of the premises then and there."

DeKok rubbed the bridge of his nose with a little finger.

"That would not have been very good. I'm sure they would have run into Henkie and me . . . or at least one of us."

Vledder grinned.

"Yes, you would have had some explaining to do, to say the least."

DeKok looked pensive.

"That's for sure, it would not have been easy."

"Any results?"

DeKok pursed his lips and nodded.

"Not at all disappointing. Certainly not. But I'll tell you later." He pulled up a chair and sat next to Vledder's desk. He was unusually fresh and cheerful after such a short night. "Tell me about Bloemendaal."

Vledder yawned again, shrugging his shoulders.

"Not much for us. There wasn't much we could do last night. Today they're going back with a dog. Perhaps they'll find something more then. Black as ink in the sand dunes at night, you know."

DeKok knew. The sand dunes along the coast formed an important part of Holland's continual battle against the sea. Without the dunes at least one third of Holland would disappear under water immediately. As a result the area was carefully protected to prevent erosion and other damage. Paths, and streetlights were only installed in a few, selected places. Holland is probably the only place in the world, thought DeKok, where one walks *up* to the beach.

"Who found her?"

Vledder took out his notebook while simultaneously powering up his computer terminal.

"It was a bit strange. At first there was some communication problem. But the cop on duty in Bloemendaal received a notification via 9-1-1. An anonymous voice made the report at exactly three minutes past eleven. The message was that the corpse of Estella Breevoorde could be found just off Seapath, in the dunes."

"They used the name?"

"Yes, and the location. Seapath is a narrow road that dead-ends into the walking path, that splits two ways from there along the edge of the dunes. One branch returns back to town along a different route and the other side leads eventually across the dunes to the beach. The nearest streetlight is at the end of Seapath. She was found on the path toward the beach, about fifty feet beyond the furthest light from the streetlight. As I said, pitch black, there."

"Go on."

"Well, the cop who took the call had heard the name Breevoorde before and he knew that a Mrs. Breevoorde lived in Bloemendaal. A nice old lady. Therefore the phone call was a bit strange and the cop thought it was a joke, or something. But he called the house anyway. She answered the phone herself and, you know how that goes at night, in a small town, he said something like: 'Gee, Ma'am, I thought you were dead.' Then . . ."

"How many cops do they have there?" interrupted DeKok.

"I don't know. But at night there are three, all constables. One in the office and two on patrol. They called a few more out of bed to cover the crime scene."

"Nice little town," said DeKok, mostly to himself.

"Yes, want me to go on?"

"Of course."

"The old lady was taken by surprise, as you may imagine. But she was immediately aware that the information must concern her daughter. She said she had been expecting her daughter since nine o'clock and was getting worried. She became even more worried when it turned out that there was no answer at Emperors Canal. Apparently she was just about ready to call the police, when the police called her."

"Poor woman."

Vledder sighed.

"I talked to her briefly, shortly after she identified the body. The poor old thing was completely out of it. She just couldn't understand why anybody could do such a thing, especially to her daughter."

"Tell me more about how they found her."

"What do you mean?"

"Condition and so on . . . come on Dick, describe the scene to me."

"Oh, yes, of course." Vledder yawned again. "She was tied to a tree."

"Tied to a tree?" DeKok was puzzled.

Vledder nodded slowly.

"When I got there, she had already been moved to the hospital. But I saw the photos. Her hands were tied behind her back and then to the tree. The ankles too, were tied together and then to the tree. Her mouth was covered with a piece of duct tape."

"Cause of death?"

"Two bullets in the neck, four in the chest and three in the belly. Two near misses . . . a scratch on the left shoulder and the upper right arm." As Vledder spoke his hands moved over the keyboard and duplicated the information from his notebook in the computer.

"Seems like overkill," said DeKok, noting that Vledder had the outline of a human figure on the screen and marked the places where the bullets had hit. He used a mole, a mouse, or a rat, or whatever they were called, to move the blinking little thing on the screen. DeKok had no use for computers.

Vledder sat back and rubbed his eyes.

"I took a close look at the body in the hospital. I think that at least two of the hits were fatal. Those immediately in the area of the heart. The rest were less life-threatening, but, according to the doctor, the cumulative effect would have been deadly. There'll be an autopsy this afternoon."

"At the hospital?"

"Yes, Bloemendaal doesn't have a police lab."

DeKok nodded his understanding.

"Shells?"

"They found seven at the scene, all from different calibers."

"Then the rest must have been revolvers, or they haven't been found yet."

"Oh, I think they were all found. The local cops have metal detectors in the cars. Probably because of all the hardware from the war that's still laying around the dunes."

"Surely the mines have all been cleared."

"Of course, but there are still a lot of spent shells and people lose things on the beach, of course."

"So, revolvers."

"You're right, of course. A revolver retains the empty shell after firing, a pistol ejects them." Vledder shook his head sadly. "Seems to me we have had this conversation before. Never thought of it last night."

DeKok looked faintly disappointed.

"You missed something else, last night."

"What?"

"Two bullets in the neck, four in the chest, three in the belly and two near misses. How many does that make?"

"Eleven."

DeKok gave him a puckish grin.

"Remember Lowee's story about the guy who wanted to buy eleven hand weapons?"

Vledder closed his eyes and groaned.

"The tall, skinny man!"

"Apparently he found a seller," grunted DeKok.

* * *

For a long time, their little corner of the busy detective room became an island of silence. Silently they stared in front of themselves, each occupied with their own thoughts.

Suddenly Vledder got up and disappeared in the direction of the bathroom. He came back a few minutes later, his hair wet and combed.

"I just put my head under the faucet," he explained grimly. "that was a little shock you gave me." He gave DeKok a meaningful look. "Shouldn't we tell our colleagues in Bloemendaal about Lowee's story?"

DeKok shook his head slowly.

"Doesn't make much sense. For the time being they can do nothing with it, anyway. Besides, we'd have to tell them the whole story."

"What about us?"

"What do you mean?"

"Is it any use to us?"

DeKok smiled. He stretched himself.

"We," he said, "are going to look for the tall, skinny guy."

"But we don't even know who he is," countered Vledder, confused.

"Come, come, my boy, we're cops, after all. We'll find out."

DeKok stood up, took a large Inter-Office envelope from the drawer of his desk and walked toward the clothes rack. Vledder followed him, a frown on his face.

"How?"

"In a round-about way," said DeKok nonchalantly. "There's more than one way to skin a cat."

"Round-about?"

"Via Hoorn," grinned DeKok.

* * *

After Zaandam, Vledder turned onto the thruway to Hoorn. After the slight curve he pressed down on the gas pedal. The old engine protested noisily, but delivered. Vledder's face was angry, his lips pressed tightly together. He was angry with himself for missing the obvious connection between the eleven gunshots and the story about eleven guns by Lowee.

He glanced at DeKok who was sprawled in the seat, thoughtfully chewing some gum. DeKok was not thinking about the case at all. He thought idly that, although the distance to Hoorn was at least twice as far as his recent trip to Purmerend, it would take almost the same time now that Vledder drove. As they passed a sign indicating 'Hoorn' DeKok reflected on what he knew about that town. Little, he realized. There had been a Count of Hoorn who, with his friend the Count of Egmont, had been beheaded by King Philip II of Spain. Later Beethoven had written the Egmont and Hoorn Overture, he seemed to remember. He smiled at a sudden memory. He was about to ask Vledder, who was a History Major, what he knew about the town, when he saw the young man's face. He decided to let it rest.

Vledder glanced at the large yellow envelope on DeKok's knees and wondered what was in it. But he was too proud to ask. As had happened so often, he had the feeling he was not part of the investigation at all. He knew that he had the same facts as DeKok, but he just could not arrange them in any order. It gave him a helpless feeling which translated into a feeling of anger, thereby allowing his anger to feed on itself. He depressed the clutch pedal and raced the engine before he released it again in a futile effort to make the old VW run faster.

DeKok heard the sudden roaring and turned toward his young friend.

"Just take it easy," he said calmly. "The day is long and . . . please keep my pension in mind. I'm not ready to join the angels." He grinned to himself. "Besides, I haven't the figure for it."

Vledder did not laugh, nor did the remark lift his spirits in any way. He stole another glance at his partner. There was a calm, satisfied look of contented certainty on DeKok's face.

Somehow it only served to irritate Vledder further. He knew that self-satisfied, smug look and he knew that DeKok was close to a solution. He could contain himself no longer.

"Whatever are we going to Hoorn for?" snarled Vledder.

DeKok pushed his lower lip forward.

"We're going to visit a woman," answered DeKok mildly. He opened the envelope and took a patient card out of it. "Her name is Mildred Visser and she lives in Loosen Park in Hoorn."

* * *

They drove around town for a while. Hoorn looked like a friendly, sleepy town. First the Dutch had closed off the former Zuyder Zee, then they had transformed more than two thirds of the area into land. Ecological concerns had spared the remaining one third and it had become the fresh-water Ijssel *Lake*, an important recreation area. A major seaport in the 17th Century, home to a large fishing fleet less than sixty years ago and now, with the closing of the enormous dike along the mouth of the inland sea and the completion of the incredible engineering feat that had made water into land, Hoorn was primarily a tourist attraction and a yachting harbor.

Vledder parked the car near the railroad station. DeKok stepped out of the car and looked around. He had fond memories of the place. It was here that he had taken the train to Amsterdam, after leaving the island on which he had been born, to start his career with the police. How long ago was that? He was still young and full of ambition. He looked at what remained of the sea. In the distance, he knew, was what remained of the island on which he had grown up. The thought made him feel melancholy.

158

Then the other memory about Hoorn again intruded itself and he smiled broadly.

"What's there to smile about," asked Vledder, irked.

"I was thinking about the last time I was in this town," replied DeKok. "It was in connection with the Weer case. It's when I met Lucienne, the friend of Jonathan Weer. Remember him?"

"Sure," said Vledder after a brief reflection. "That was when almost an entire family was killed. Didn't it start with a dead woman in an alley?"*

"Right. She was dressed in a fur coat."

"Yes, yes," prompted Vledder impatiently. "What about it?"

"At the time, on my way here, I was on the train with Lucienne, without knowing it was her. I fell asleep admiring her legs. I remember thinking at the time that if you had known, you would have recommended early retirement for me."

Vledder snorted and turned on his heel. He walked away in the direction of Loosen Park.

* * *

She seemed sweet and a little fragile. Her blue-green eyes focused a puzzled look on the faces of the two Inspectors.

"Police?"

DeKok bowed and gave her a charming smile.

"We came all the way from Amsterdam."

She cocked her head at him and smiled thinly.

"This is supposed to be an honor for me?"

"Hardly," said DeKok pleasantly.

---

* See: *DeKok and the Careful Killer.*

She opened the door wider and allowed the men to step inside. The small room was a cozy, friendly place full of knick-knacks and a lot of lace coverings on windows, chairs and tables. She pointed at some chairs with straw seats, grouped around a round table.

"How can I help you, gentlemen?"

DeKok hesitated for a moment. He did not want to hurt this friendly, fragile old lady. He pulled out a card and showed it to her.

"Do you know what this is?" he asked.

She turned and picked up her glasses from a sideboard. She looked at the card and then shook her head.

"I don't know."

DeKok read:

"Mildred Visser, Loosen Park, Hoorn. That's you, isn't it?"

She nodded.

"Yes."

DeKok tapped the card.

"About five years ago you were a patient of Doctor Beaumonde, a psychiatrist in Amsterdam. This is his patient card."

Deep in thought, she stroked the lace table cloth with her fingers.

"That's right," she said finally. "I was his patient. A fine man. Understanding. I had some difficulties at that time." She removed her glasses. "A matter of repressed emotional upheaval. That's what the doctor called it."

"In other words," said DeKok, "an unhappy event in the past that even in later years, you had not learned to live with. And something you did not like to be reminded of."

She did not answer at once. With a shaky hand she patted her thin, gray hair in place.

"It was . . . at the time, it was an embarrassing situation. I . . . eh, in Hoorn I'm well regarded, to a certain extent. People know me. That's why I didn't want anybody here to know."

DeKok leaned closer.

"And that was worth something to you?"

She sighed deeply.

"The sins of the past are the ghosts of today. It did cost me a lot of money to keep the affair secret."

"Why didn't you go to the police?"

She gave him a sad smile and shook her head.

"In that case I might as well have taken an ad in the paper."

DeKok was about to protest strongly, but thought better of it. He did not want to antagonize Mildred Visser. As much as possible, he wanted to preserve the right mood. He stood up from his chair and stood next to her. Carefully, gently, he placed a hand on her shoulder.

"It's all over now," he said softly, encouragingly.

She looked up at him, tears in her eyes.

"You know?"

DeKok nodded slowly. There was a compassionate look in his eyes.

"Why did you send the warnings?"

16

Vledder was speechless. It took almost a minute before he was able to make a sound.

"*You . . . you* sent those letters?"

Mildred Visser nodded slowly, reluctantly.

"One by mail. The other one I pushed under the door."

Vledder swallowed.

"And for that you went all the way to Amsterdam?"

She folded her hands and placed them on the table.

"Dying," she said soberly, "is more than the closing of a book that no longer absorbs you. I've always been troubled by it. I have said so. I abhor violence."

The young Inspector was flabbergasted.

"And you . . . you *knew* that Estella Beaumonde was about to die?"

There was a sad smile on her face.

"We agreed."

"Who is *we*?"

Mildred Visser avoided Vledder's eyes. She darted a quick look over her shoulder at DeKok, as if looking for support. DeKok intervened.

"You're not allowed to mention the other names, isn't that so?"

She shook her head.

"We're not allowed. We swore together . . . on the Bible."

DeKok nodded sympathetically.

"You sent those two letters, those warnings, anonymously because you didn't want the others to know that basically you didn't agree."

She made a helpless gesture.

"I had already agreed and I didn't want to break my promise. I just hoped fervently that Estella wouldn't show up . . . so she would not have to endure the terrible ordeal."

"But it happened."

Mildred did not answer. She lowered her head to the table. Her bony shoulders shook. DeKok looked down on her. He saw the pink skin through the thin, gray hair and felt a deep pity for this old woman. He understood the pain in her soul.

"You were waiting for her in Bloemendaal?"

She waved shaky hands.

"I didn't know anything about the plans. Everything had been arranged. I just had to be there. They said it was necessary. It was revenge for all the terrible things Estella had done. We all suffered from her." Tears came down her cheeks and splattered on the spotless, lace tablecloth. "I will never forget her eyes, that night . . . so big, so brown . . . so full of fear. It was just as if she did not understand what was happening. That's how she looked. I could never have gone through with it, if they had not blindfolded her."

"But you did?"

Mildred Visser sighed deeply. She seemed to have regained a little bit of self-control. With the back of her hand she wiped the tears from her eyes.

"We did it," she said, emphasizing every word with a nod. "One by one. Estella Beaumonde had lost the right to live, they said. They all said it."

164

A silence fell. DeKok looked at the lace curtains in front of the window. The trees outside showed some early, vigorous green. There were crocuses under the trees and few starlings fought over a bread crust. Inside, on the marble mantelpiece an old-fashioned pendulum clock ticked away the minutes.

DeKok let the minutes go by. Consciously. He had an inborn feeling for the dramatic. Then he went back to his chair and sat down. In front of him was the large, yellow envelope. Slowly, he pushed it in Mildred's direction.

"In here," he said gravely, "are thirteen patient's cards . . . thirteen people. You are one of them and two of them are dead. You have a choice out of ten. One of the ten is a tall, skinny man. No doubt you know exactly who I mean. You don't have to speak his name." He took an old-fashioned fountain pen from his pocket and placed it next to the envelope. "My colleague and I will turn away. Take the cards out of the envelope and put an X on the card belonging to the man I'm looking for. Just in the upper right hand corner. That's all. Then you put the cards back in the envelope."

She stared at him.

"And if I refuse?"

DeKok shrugged his shoulders carelessly, but he looked somber.

"My fate is in your hands. Your refusal will severely hamper my investigations."

Mildred Visser accepted the envelope and took out the cards.

"He's a noble human being. Sincere and honest. He was a great support to us all."

DeKok did not react. He motioned toward Vledder. Both men stood up and turned their backs.

* * *

165

They walked back to the railroad station, to where their car was parked. DeKok placed his hand on Vledder's arm.

"I think I owe you an explanation," he apologized. "I understand full well that you were, to say the least, a bit peeved this morning. Very understandable . . . the human thing to be. I could have explained sooner, but I wanted to wait until after we had talked to Mildred Visser. There was always the possibility I could have been wrong."

Vledder grimaced.

"Well, you gave me a number of surprises."

They drove off and DeKok gave directions.

"Near the Zuyder Zee Museum is an excellent restaurant. I'll buy."

"Buying me off?"

"If you will."

* * *

After driving through a number of picturesque, narrow streets, they stopped in front of the *Old Pepperhouse*, a former spice warehouse of the Dutch East Indies Company, dating from the 1600s, now converted to a restaurant. DeKok hoisted himself out of the car and looked up at the elegant double-stair gable. Vledder stood next to him, ignoring the gorgeous architecture of the 17th Century building.

"Why Mildred Visser?"

DeKok did not answer. He walked into the restaurant and found a place near the window. He placed the yellow envelope on the table next to his place setting.

Vledder joined him. DeKok waited until the waiter had brought a glass of cognac for him and iced tea for Vledder. After a first, careful sip, DeKok addressed Vledder.

"Too bad you're driving. This cognac is excellent."

"Why Mildred Visser?" repeated Vledder stubbornly.

DeKok gave in.

"From the start of this investigation we have been confused," he said, "by the emotional ties between Josephine and the first two victims. It even led to her arrest. I confess that it took a little while before I was convinced of her innocence, or rather, that her relationships with the men had nothing to do with the case. The only important link was the common phone number in the pocket agendas of the victims ... the phone number of psychiatrist Charles Paul Beaumonde. But the man was dead ... for more than five years. I don't know where he finally wound up ... in Heaven, or in Hell ... but I've never seen a murderer come from either place."

Vledder laughed.

"But no matter which way you look at it ... because of that phone number the victims were connected to that house on Emperors Canal."

"Very good," said DeKok and took another sip from his drink. Then he raised an index finger in the air.

"Very good," he repeated. "That opened the question ... connected to whom? ... who was still alive? The only person who could be considered for that was Estella Beaumonde, the young widow of the psychiatrist. The phone number had not been changed." He paused and nodded his head at the waiter who had approached in response to the raised finger. "The second important question we had to ask ourselves was ... what gave the killer such power over his, or her, victims that they could be directed to a specific spot by a simple cross on an Amsterdam street map. There was only one answer I could think of. Blackmail! But what was used to blackmail the victims?" He pointed a finger at Vledder. "You gave me the idea. You told me that Beaumonde used hypnosis in his therapy in order to bring so-called repressed emotional experiences to the surface. Then I learned from Estella that her husband called the safe in his office *Pandora's Box* and I knew where the psychiatrist kept his patient's secrets."

"In the old safe."

DeKok nodded and drained his glass. Silently he stared out of the window.

"Go on," prodded Vledder.

"Doctor Beaumonde," continued DeKok, "must have had a strange sense of humor. *Pandora's Box* seems a bitter mockery. That's where he kept all the misery, ailments and pain of his clients."

Vledder, always ready to state the obvious, had to do so this time as well.

"The confidential revelations, whether under hypnosis, or not, from a patient to his, or her, psychiatrist."

"Yes," said DeKok. "And I started to wonder what sort of secrets the safe contained . . . about who . . . how they had been classified."

Vledder grinned suddenly.

"And so that safe had to be opened."

"It was a special experience to see Handy Henkie at work. He stroked that old safe as if it was a long-lost girlfriend and it took just a few minutes before the heavy door was opened."

"What was in it?"

"Tapes . . . audio tapes . . . those little ones."

"Micro cassettes," suggested Vledder.

"Whatever. In any case, the cassettes had been used to record the conversations between the doctor and his patients. No doubt he listened to them afterward to help him in deciding on a course of treatment."

"You didn't take the tapes?"

DeKok shook his head.

"No I left them in the safe. Henkie and I moved them out and in again. It worked very smoothly. I only recorded which tapes were missing."

Vledder was surprised.

"How could you do that? It seems more difficult to determine the missing tapes than to just inventory what is there."

"Ah, but I used the patient's cards on the desk. From everything I saw, it seems that Doctor Beaumonde was a careful, methodical man. Therefore I presumed that there had be a tape, or tapes, for every patient on the cards in the box."

"And?"

"I was right. There was at least one tape for every patient on the cards . . . with the exception of thirteen."

"Thirteen?"

"Yes, I was left with thirteen cards for which there were no tapes."

Vledder pointed at the yellow envelope.

"These thirteen."

DeKok sighed.

"Of which two are dead . . . Jan-Willem Hoffman and Alex Peetersen. That leaves . . . eleven patients."

Vledder caught his breath.

"And a tall, skinny man who asked Little Lowee about buying eleven hand weapons."

DeKok nodded thoughtfully.

"And . . . Estella Beaumonde, who has been shot eleven times."

The waiter served soup. Both ate in silence. Suddenly Vledder spoke.

"Why did we first go to Mildred Visser, here in Hoorn?"

DeKok put down his spoon.

"The first letter Estella received was post-marked in Hoorn. Among the eleven there was only one patient who lived in Hoorn ... Mildred Visser."

Vledder shook his head.

"That's how easy the life of a detective can be."

The meal was excellent. When the Inspectors pushed their chairs back, they were pleasantly sated. The waiter cleared the table and Vledder opened the yellow envelope.

"I want to know who the tall, skinny man is."

He took the cards out of the envelope and looked at them. DeKok watched with interest.

"What's the matter?" asked DeKok, when he saw the expression on his partner's face.

"She's tricked us."

"What?"

"Mildred Visser ... *all* the cards are marked."

17

After DeKok had paid the hefty check, they left the restaurant. DeKok took another look at the old facades. He liked Hoorn. Not as much as his beloved Amsterdam, but Hoorn, too, was full of fond memories. As a small boy he and his father had walked through the narrow streets and his father always bought him a treat . . . a piece of sausage, a bag of chips, a herring, or a smoked mackerel. He was still in a dreamy mood as he reached the VW and wriggled into the seat. Vledder started the engine and looked aside.

"Want to go back?"

"Where to?"

"Mildred Visser, of course."

DeKok smiled to himself.

"She tricked us, but good."

Vledder was impatient.

"Are we going back there, or what?"

DeKok shook his head, still smiling.

"Let her be," he said soothingly. "We're going back to Amsterdam." He hoisted himself upright in the seat. "I think that Mildred at first just put a cross on the right card, but then she thought better of it. There was no way to remove the mark she had made, of course."

Vledder grinned maliciously.

"So then she marked *all* the cards."

DeKok laughed while he looked approvingly at the mint the restaurant had served with the coffee.

"I can admire that," chuckled DeKok. "It takes a certain amount of wit to come to that solution. She isn't all that young anymore . . . and she didn't have a lot of time." He held the yellow envelope in the air. "Anyway," he added, "at least we can be certain of one thing . . . the tall skinny man is one of those here."

"One of the eleven . . . still alive."

With one hand DeKok stuffed the mint in his mouth and with the other he shook the cards out of the envelope.

"I took a good look at them before. Dr. Beaumonde made the same codes and marks on all of them. Apparently all thirteen patients have the same kind of disorder . . . the same kind of psychic difficulties."

"Repressed emotional behavior."

"Yes," nodded DeKok. "We know about Jan-Willem. That in his younger years he was most probably involved in a rape. A rape with horrible consequences. Mildred Visser talked about a humiliating experience that she wanted to keep secret. I have an idea that all thirteen have something in their past of which they are less than proud and would like to keep hidden . . . something that will not stand the light of day in our honest, respectable society."

Vledder grimaced.

"You really think we live in an honest, respectable society?"

DeKok nodded with conviction.

"We, police officers," he said in a didactic tone of voice, "often forget that. In our profession we touch upon crime so frequently, that sometimes we get the overwhelming feeling that

172

the world only consists of bad people. I've heard the theory that at least twenty percent of any population is bad. But I don't agree. That would mean that one out of every five people you meet is a criminal, or a potential criminal. A depressing thought by itself. No, I think that, happily, most people are respectable citizens with a conventional morality."

Vledder snorted.

"And that atmosphere creates blackmailers."

DeKok did not react. While Vledder urged the recalcitrant VW in the direction of Amsterdam, DeKok studied the cards again. Finally he spoke.

"Of those that are left," he said, "six are women. That leaves us five men. Fred Prins discovered from the restaurant waitress that we are looking for a tall, skinny man and Lowee confirmed that, in a way. Therefore, I think, we can safely assume that he's older than fifty. Then, when I check the men, only two can be considered . . . one is Baptiste Verbruggen and a man by the name of Frederick Dender. The others are too young."

"Why are you concentrating on the tall, skinny guy?" Vledder glanced meaningfully at the cards on DeKok's knees. "After all, they're all involved."

"True," said DeKok, "but he's clearly the leader, the instigator."

"Of what?"

"Of the patients gathering . . . the court of thirteen . . . or whatever you want to call it . . . kangaroo court, maybe. He was the man who was with Alex Peetersen. He was the man who asked about buying eleven weapons . . . and found them. At the same time he is, according to Mildred Visser, a noble, honest and sincere person, a great support to them all." He made a violent gesture that caused the cards to slide of knees. "I can't help it. That man intrigues me."

173

Vledder thought for a few seconds.

"Do you think he knows why, and by who, Peetersen, Hoffman and Red Bakker were killed?"

DeKok sighed and shrugged his shoulders.

"Maybe. In any case he had a motive, or thought he did, for killing Estella Beaumonde."

* * *

Vledder parked the VW on the dock over the Damrak, behind the station. They entered the station-house through the back door. When they walked into the detective room, Fred Prins looked up and then met them halfway. There was a worried look on the young man's face.

"Commissaris Buitendam has asked for you several times. He wants to talk to you urgently." Then Prins winked at Vledder. "Radio off again, eh?"

DeKok growled something.

"What?" asked Prins politely.

"I don't solve cases being tied to his apron strings," repeated DeKok.

He threw the yellow envelope in a desk drawer and stomped out of the room. At the end of the corridor he walked into the commissarial office.

Buitendam immediately rose from his chair.

"I want to speak with you most urgently," said the Chief.

"I heard," said DeKok.

"Last night you sent Inspector Vledder to Bloemendaal."

"Yes, I did."

"Why?"

"Because I was interested in a woman who had been killed in the dunes nearby."

"What sort of interest?"

"She most likely plays a part in the murders I'm investigating."

"She's involved?"

"Possibly."

Commissaris Buitendam made an impatient gesture.

"My counterpart in Bloemendaal called. His Inspector has a feeling that you know more about the background of the murder of that woman. More than Vledder told them, for certain."

DeKok pursed his lips.

"Mmm," he said, "they should hang on to that feeling."

The pale face of the Commissaris was getting red.

"Your . . . eh, your *obstinate* behavior has already caused me some difficulty with my colleague Dietinga in Deyssel Street. I do *not* want difficulties with Bloemendaal."

DeKok rubbed the bridge of his nose with a little finger.

"If they're just a little patient . . . just a little longer . . . I'll serve them the perpetrators of that murder on a silver platter."

The commissarial face was angry.

"Why *should* they be patient?"

For a moment DeKok pressed his lips together as if he was not going to say anything else.

"Because," he said finally, slowly, "I don't want some hot-shot of a provincial Commissaris to run rough shod all over my investigation."

The Commissaris was speechless. With a shaking hand he pointed at the door. DeKok turned resignedly and went to the door. Just before he left the room, the Commissaris found his voice.

"OUT!" roared the Commissaris.

* * *

"I heard," laughed Vledder. "I was waiting just inside the door here and I could hear him yell. Why *don't* you two get along?"

DeKok shook his head, as if to clear it.

"Sometimes that man is incapable of having a normal conversation. If he gets the slightest inkling that the authority or dignity of police chiefs is impaired, whether real or imagined, he'll send you from the room." He smiled without joy. "It's one way to resolve an argument, of course, you simply send your opponent away."

Meanwhile they had crossed the room to their own desks. Vledder sat down and with almost the same movement activated his computer terminal. With a few quick sentences he summarized the interview with Mildred Visser. Then he reached for DeKok's desk to retrieve the yellow envelope. DeKok stopped him with a gesture.

"Are we doing something else, tonight?" asked Vledder.

DeKok nodded, a determined look on his face.

"Yes, and we better hurry. There's little time. As soon as the cops in Bloemendaal get a whiff that Dr. Beaumonde's former patients are involved in the murder, half the Bloemendaal force . . ."

"All six of them," interrupted Vledder.

". . . will descend upon us," continued DeKok, ignoring the interruption. ". . . and we can't do anything without stumbling over them. Just to be on the safe side, to prevent any unnecessary trouble, these cards will have to get back to Emperors canal as soon as possible."

"First let me copy the names."

"All right," said DeKok and handed him the envelope.

It did not take long and with a happy smile, knowing his records were up-to-date, Vledder handed back the envelope.

"How are we going to get them back?" asked Vledder.

DeKok winked.

"I still have Handy Henkie's handy little door persuader. I may not be able to open a safe but, thanks to Henkie, a house door has no secrets for me."

"DeKok!" yelled a detective over the noise of the room.

They looked up and saw the detective point in their direction. A tall, skinny man followed the direction of the pointing finger.

The visitor was about fifty years old with wavy gray hair and expensively dressed in a dark-grey suit. He approached DeKok's desk with outstretched hand.

"Frederick Dender," he said in a bass voice by way of introduction. "You, of course, are Inspector DeKok."

DeKok looked at the man while he shook the outstretched hand.

"Indeed," admitted DeKok.

"I'm turning myself in," said the man with a broad smile.

"What for?"

"For my part in the murder of Estella Beaumonde."

* * *

It took a few seconds before DeKok had his breathing back under control. The sudden appearance of the man had literally taken his breath away. He pointed at the chair next to his desk.

"Please sit down. To be absolutely frank ... I'm taken aback. I was convinced we'd have to hunt you down."

Dender made a careless gesture.

"One must know when the battle is lost. When Mildred Visser called me this afternoon to inform me about your visit, I understood that your appearance would only be a matter of time."

"There are nine others."

Frederick Dender waved that remark away.

177

"I know my personal responsibility. And as leader of our group I will not evade it. The participation of the others is less . . . perhaps not in execution, but in concept, the planning."

DeKok cocked his head at his strange visitor.

"It was your decision that Estella Beaumonde had to die?"

Dender shook his head.

"The proposal was mine. The final decision was made by all of us . . . unanimously."

DeKok scratched the back of his neck.

"As I understand it, there was some sort of agreement, an accord . . . a deadly accord to kill Estella Beaumonde."

"You are correct."

DeKok snorted contemptuously.

"On what basis?"

Dender smiled again.

"On the basis of her criminal behavior toward us. She deserved to die."

DeKok jumped up. His face was red.

"And you just decided . . . just like that! A little party, perhaps? A few drinks and then . . . come on, let's kill her." His voice dripped with sarcasm. "Where in Heaven's name did you find the courage?"

Frederick Dender pressed his lips together during DeKok's tirade. Then he answered.

"We *had* that courage," he said coldly. "It was the courage of justice . . . in Heaven's name. There was no other way out. Estella Beaumonde blackmailed us all."

"And?"

"She was systematically killing us all, murdering us."

DeKok gave him an astonished look.

"How did you decide that?"

The tall, skinny man raised his thumb and forefinger.

"Jan-Willem Hoffman . . . Alexander Peetersen."

DeKok swallowed.

"*She* committed those murders?"

Dender nodded. His face was serious.

"I was a witness. I saw her do it."

18

Frederick Dender moved in his chair.

"Perhaps it is better," he began calmly, considering, "that I first give you some of the background." He closed his eyes to help himself concentrate. "About seven years ago I became a patient of Dr. Beaumonde. I had a psychological problem that was a liability to me in my capacity as Managing Director of a large firm. There were times when I was unable to do my work at all. Friends told me about Dr. Beaumonde at Emperors Canal and about the remarkable results he obtained through the use of hypnosis. I was indeed helped by the therapy and became interested in his methods. One day he discussed with me the possibilities of group therapy. He had a number of patients who all suffered from more or less the same problems and because of similar causes. He wanted to bring these people together in regular group sessions."

"The group of thirteen."

Frederick Dender nodded pensively.

"The beginning was a bit hesitant, a bit strange. But as time went on, the group therapy helped us to become friends. The bonds became strong enough that we decided to keep on meeting, even after the death of Dr. Beaumonde. It helped us."

"Did that happen often?"

"We used to gather roughly once every two months. Usually on neutral ground . . . not in our homes, but somewhere in the country, a restaurant where I could rent a private room."

"You were the leader right from the start?"

Dender shrugged and smiled wanly.

"There was never an official vote. It just sort of happened. Everybody seemed to agree that I was the right man for the job."

"When did the blackmail start?"

"About a year after Dr. Beaumonde died. One of us was sent a street map of Amsterdam on which was indicated the place of a meeting. He was urged to appear because he would learn some important information."

"Who was that?"

"Jan-Willem Hoffman. He was almost definitely the first one to be approached that way. What is strange, is that, although there was a comfortable, confidential atmosphere in our group, Jan-Willem kept quiet about it . . . at least in the beginning. He just paid the blackmail. The same, I must admit, was also true for me. Only last year did the subject come up during one of our meetings. I think it was Mildred Visser who first broached it. Then it was discovered that all members of the group had been paying substantial amounts in blackmail, all along. In all cases the blackmail was based on confidential information we had divulged to Dr. Beaumonde."

"Who was the blackmailer?"

Frederick Dender made a sweeping gesture.

"Estella Beaumonde. As far as I know, she never kept it a secret. She signed her letters with 'Estella' and appeared in person to receive her blood money. That always happened in the evening, after dark, in some lonely and quiet place, she apparently had carefully selected in advance."

"So, what did you decide to do?"

"Jan-Willem wanted to go to the police. One night, after he had a few, he finally gathered enough courage to do just that. He went to Warmoes Street station. I don't know why he picked that one. Possibly it was close. But that night there was no detective available and the uniformed police officer told him to come back later. So his complaint was never registered, as far as I know."

"And?"

Dender rubbed his chin, a thoughtful look in his eyes, as if reliving the moment.

"I advised him against going back the next day. I told him that the police is full of leaks as well. I've read things about that. I suggested to Jan-Willem that he simply stop paying. The next time he was summoned, he would tell her that he was not paying another cent and that the rest of the group was of the same opinion."

DeKok looked somber.

"Bad advice. It became his death warrant."

Dender sighed.

"We read about it in the paper and called an emergency meeting. Nobody wanted to believe it. We thought that Jan-Willem had simply fallen victim to a murderer, any murderer. We simply found it impossible to believe that Estella Beaumonde was capable of such a deed. In order to be sure, we decided that Peetersen would react the same way, during *his* next meeting with Estella."

"Why Peetersen?"

"We did not control the order. We had to wait until we heard from Estella to tell us where to meet. Jan-Willem was simply the next in line. Peetersen was next."

"He, too, was going to tell her that he was through paying and had the support of the group?"

"Exactly, that was the plan. Alex Peetersen wanted me to come with him to the meeting place, but I was afraid that Estella might not show in that case. We decided that Alex would first proceed to the meeting place and I would be close behind."

"So you met at the *Lotus* restaurant and left from there?"

"It was close by."

"What happened?"

Frederick Dender hesitated. He seemed to have trouble continuing. He swallowed several times. DeKok looked at Vledder and the young Inspector quickly placed a glass of water in front of the visitor. Dender looked grateful and took a sip. It seemed to steady him.

"When Alex had been gone for about ten minutes," continued the tall, skinny man, "I left the restaurant and, via Bantam Street and New Knight Street, I soon reached the area at Lastage Road." He paused and took another sip of water. He had paled visibly since entering. "I saw them on an open spot. I was barely thirty feet away. I could see everything in the light of a nearby light pole. Suddenly Estella took a handgun from her purse and shot Alex. There were three shots. Alex collapsed. It happened so fast and so unexpectedly that I was unable to react. I was paralyzed. My legs refused to function. I stood nailed to the ground and watched Estella flee the scene." He wiped the back of his hand over his eyes. "I have never in my life been so shocked."

DeKok gave him a long, searching look.

"Then, when you regained your senses, so to speak, you decided Estella had to die?"

Dender nodded slowly.

"Yes, I decided to propose it to the group."

"Why did you not go to the police? You were an eye-witness. With your statement the case would have been solved quickly."

Dender spread his hands.

"I'm a lawyer," he said dully. "I'm not a member of the bar and I don't practice law, but I have a law degree. Perhaps because of that I should believe in justice." He shook his head sadly. "But for that I lack the faith and the belief."

DeKok looked at him evenly.

"I'm a cop . . . more than thirty years. I *have* faith and trust in the Law . . . still."

Frederick Dender sighed elaborately.

"Then you're a man to be envied." It sounded a bit snide. "But what else can you do? You only have to bring the truth to light. That's all. What others do with the truth you discover is not your responsibility. The Judge-Advocate has the right to dismiss the case . . . or to plea-bargain. In other words, let it disappear, or apply a slap on the wrist. And believe me, he uses that right every chance he gets. It reduces the calendar and the workloads of the Courts." He raised an arm in the air. "The members of the judicial system hardly remember the meaning of the word justice." He smiled tauntingly. "And as far as the sentences are concerned . . . the actual punishment to be imposed . . . that's just another farce. Our present-day prisons and institutions resemble country clubs, hotels with a twenty-four hours a day checking in and checking out . . . the prisoners practically come and go as they please."

DeKok did not react. The arguments of his visitor hurt him, because he knew different. For a moment he contemplated arguing the point, but then rejected the idea. It would be pointless. He leaned closer.

"And that is why you decided to take the law in your own hands?"

Dender looked up.

"That's what we decided," he said simply.

"You bought eleven weapons and waited for Estella in Bloemendaal."

"Yes."

"You took her into the dunes and tied her to a tree and all of you shot her."

"All of us wanted to participate in the execution."

"And the weapons?"

"I gathered them up after the execution and dumped them in the North Sea."

DeKok stood up. The conversation with Frederick Dender had exhausted him. He paced up and down for a few minutes, trying to banish the dull throbbing in his head. He stopped in front of the window and stared outside for a while. Then he turned around. His face was expressionless.

"Mr. Dender . . . you may leave. You should keep yourself available to the police, however. I will have a surprise for you."

"What sort of surprise?"

DeKok shook his head slowly, sadly.

"Not a pleasant one, I'm afraid."

19

After Frederick Dender had left, DeKok sank back in his chair. He leaned backward and with a painful grimace he placed his tired feet on the desk. He looked tired and exhausted. The fight against crime became harder as he grew older. There was so much ignorance, distrust and misunderstanding regarding the authorities, the Law. And he represented the Law. He was a representative of the Law and his duties were to uphold the Law. But the Law was seldom just right or wrong, black or white, one way or the other. More and more he was inclined to look at it as varying shades of gray. After all, he concluded, the Law deals with people.

Vledder sat down on the edge of his desk.

"Well, now everything is solved," he laughed, relieved. "Estella Beaumonde blackmailed thirteen of her husband's former patients. When the patients became obstreperous, rebelled and refused to pay any more, she shot them. Possibly as a warning to the others."

DeKok nodded.

"Very neat, but it had the opposite effect. The patients grew closer together and condemned Estella to death. Together they carried out the sentence."

Vledder made a grand gesture.

"All we have to do now is to give the names of Mildred Visser, Frederick Dender and the other nine to the police in Bloemendaal. They'll be happy . . . case closed."

DeKok grinned mockingly.

"Fini . . . done . . . curtain."

Vledder heard the cynical tone and was amazed.

"What else do you want?"

* * *

DeKok took his legs off the desk and stood up. He placed a hand on Vledder's shoulder.

"You've always been a great support to me, Dick," he said solemnly. "In this case, too. I'm very grateful for that."

Vledder grimaced, embarrassed. The Dutch are not demonstrative people.

"Don't be so dramatic."

DeKok shook his head.

"I mean it, Dick. I'm serious. And . . . I hope I can count on you again."

Vledder moved from embarrassment to irritation, DeKok's tone was getting on his nerves.

"Of course you can count on me," he said sharply. "What's all this nonsense, anyway?"

DeKok rubbed his chin thoughtfully.

"I'll be gone for a day, two days at most. During that time I don't want to be reached. If anybody asks for me, for instance the cops in Bloemendaal, or the Commissaris, you'll find some excuse." He picked up the large yellow envelope and held it in the air. "You delete these names from your thing there and, as far as you're concerned, I'm the only one who knows these thirteen names. You understand? You don't know them. I don't want Bloemendaal to know either." With the envelope under one arm

188

he walked over to the coat rack and grabbed his coat. He turned toward Vledder who had sat down behind his terminal.

There was a tired smile on DeKok's face.

"Don't worry about a thing, I'll contact you."

Vledder looked up, while his hands flew over the keyboard. There was a puzzled look on his face.

"What are you going to do?"

"Arrange a murder," said DeKok cryptically and headed for the door.

* * *

Detective-Inspector DeKok returned exactly forty-eight hours later. He stepped into the busy detective room at Warmoes Street station and was immediately noticed by Vledder. Vledder saw the nervous, tense expression on his partner's face. Quickly he walked over and helped DeKok out of his coat.

"Any problems?" asked DeKok.

"Hardly any," replied Vledder, shaking his head.

"Did you do what I asked?"

"Yes, everything is ready . . . including the four unmarked cars. Believe me, that was the hardest part to arrange."

"Have they been situated?"

Vledder pointed at a map on his desk.

"Here at East Dock Quay, near the training vessel *Pollux*. Exactly as you asked, in a square, mixed in with the other cars and with the headlights aimed at the center."

DeKok smiled gratefully.

"Does Inspector Riggelink know what it's all about?"

Vledder shook his head.

"No, he was surprised to learn he needed a bullet-proof vest."

"What about the others?"

"Fred Prins and Emil Bower know what we're after. They each have a car. I gave them bullet-proof vests as well."

DeKok walked toward one of the interrogation rooms where Riggelink was waiting. The Inspector had difficulty buttoning his coat over the bullet-proof vest. DeKok gave him an encouraging smile.

"It's mostly a precaution," he said. "I don't want there to be the slightest risk." Behind his back Vledder grimaced. He knew that DeKok never carried a weapon and had been known to take inordinate risks when confronting armed, or potentially dangerous opponents.

Riggelink twirled the ends of his moustache.

"What exactly is going to happen?"

"With a little luck this will be the conclusion of the blackmail case you were almost involved with, some time ago."

Riggelink looked a question.

"The man who came in to report blackmail and then changed his mind."

"Oh, yes. Nothing came of it."

"Something will this time, I hope. Tonight at exactly ten o'clock you'll meet a woman in the parking lot near *Pollux*. You have an appointment with that woman."

Riggelink grinned.

"I didn't know anything about that, what's more, my wife doesn't either."

DeKok smiled.

"That's right. But don't worry. The woman you're meeting also doesn't know the man she has the appointment with." He waved impatiently. "I'll tell you later how it all fits together. We're running out of time. But let me warn you, she doesn't have any amorous intentions. On the contrary, the woman is extremely dangerous and determined to kill you."

Riggelink uneasily rubbed the back of his head.

190

"How?"

DeKok sighed.

"She will be carrying a purse and in that purse is a pistol. Don't have any illusions about that, she knows how to handle it. What you have to do is this: a few minutes before ten you stand in the center of the parking lot, on a spot Vledder will show you. I'm giving you a folded Amsterdam street map and you keep that in your left hand. As soon as you see the woman, you wave with the map and start walking toward her. Not in a rush, but calm, nonchalant. As soon as you're close enough, you rip her purse out of her hands. Do it right. Be careful. Don't give her a chance to get a hand on that pistol."

Riggelink grinned nervously.

"Now I know why Vledder insisted on the vest."

DeKok raised a finger in the air.

"Just throw the purse away, far away, anywhere . . . we'll find it, later. Then you try to overpower the woman. As soon as you have your hands on the purse, assistance will come from all sides." He looked at his watch, it was almost nine. "It seems best if you all take your positions now." He compared his watch with the large clock on the wall. "I'll be along . . . with Frederick Dender."

"He's coming too?"

DeKok grinned falsely.

"This entire performance is partly because of him."

* * *

It was fifteen minutes to ten.

DeKok was behind the wheel of an old Opel Rekord, borrowed from headquarters. Frederick Dender was seated next to him and was still recovering from the shock of having been a passenger in a car driven by DeKok. The parking lot was quiet and deserted. The three masts of *Pollux* were outlined against the night sky and the reflected lights from buildings across the water. A few tourist buses were parked near the ship, their drivers no doubt asleep in a nearby hotel and their passengers on a tour of the Red Light District.

DeKok looked around. He knew he was in the right spot. Across from him, he knew, was the car with Vledder and Riggelink. Off to his left was Emil Bower and Fred Prins was somewhere off to his right. Dender moved uneasily in his seat.

"What are we doing here?"

His voice sounded tentative, unsure of himself.

"Practicing justice," said DeKok sarcastically.

"A scurrilous attempt at humor," snorted Dender.

DeKok ignored the remark. He peered through the windshield. Riggelink had emerged from his car and walked toward the center of the lot.

DeKok looked at his watch. Seven to ten. He felt his heartbeat increase. The arteries in his neck seemed to swell to double their size. It had to succeed. He had planned everything most carefully and she just *had* to appear. With the all-important murder weapon in her purse.

Minutes seemed to pass like centuries.

Suddenly, despite everything still unexpected, a woman appeared from the left. A small figure on high heels. Hesitantly she approached the center of the lot. Riggelink walked toward her, waving his map.

DeKok heard Dender pant next to him. The man was shocked. He leaned forward, his hands against the windshield.

"That's Estella . . . that's impossible . . . that's Estella . . . that's impossible . . . it shouldn't happen this way . . . it's Estella . . ."

There was fear and astonishment in his voice.

With a wild movement he tried to get out of the car. DeKok took hold of him with an iron grip. People were always surprised at the power in DeKok's old body. Dender was helpless.

They watched as Riggelink made a sudden move for the purse. The attack succeeded partially. The purse fell on the ground and rolled away just a few feet. At the same time headlights flicked on from four sides. A furious struggle developed in the sharp light from the cars.

Fred Prins came running from the right. His heavy footsteps thundered across the quiet lot.

Scratching, on hands and knees, the woman tried to reach the purse. Prins kicked the purse away and fell heavily on top of the woman.

DeKok let go of Dender. They got out of the car and approached. Riggelink and Bower pulled the woman from underneath Fred Prins and helped her to her feet.

DeKok looked at her for a second and then, with a quick movement, he pulled the black wig from her head. Vledder swallowed.

"Felix," he exclaimed, "Felix Beaumonde."

DeKok looked aside at the tall, skinny man. Dender's face had lost all color. He swayed for a moment and then, before anyone could support him, Frederick Dender lost consciousness and fell to the ground.

20

DeKok had invited the colleagues who, as he called it, had participated in the denouement, for a small party at his house. Vledder was almost a regular guest at these occasions and Fred Prins, who had more or less taken over from Robert Antoine Dijk, had been invited often. Emil Bower had once or twice participated in the gracious hospitality offered by Mrs. DeKok. It was Bert Riggelink's first visit.

"What a handsome moustache," admired Mrs. DeKok when she was introduced to Riggelink. She immediately won Riggelink's heart.

DeKok laughed and Riggelink still blushed as he sat down.

DeKok appeared relaxed and jovial. Now that the case was closed, all emotions had disappeared. As usual, he had obtained an extraordinarily fine bottle of cognac to accompany the delicacies prepared by Mrs. DeKok.

None of the men was surprised to see the platters of food. The Dutch seldom drink without eating and Mrs. DeKok's reputation as an excellent cook was common knowledge in Warmoes Street.

Of course, Vledder, impetuous as always, could not contain his curiosity. Impatiently he peppered DeKok with questions. He knew DeKok longer, and better, than any of the others and was determined to learn everything there was to know. Someday, he hoped, he would be able to take DeKok's place in the esteem of his colleagues.* On the other hand he hoped fervently that he would be able to work with DeKok for a long time to come. Now he leaned closer, the magnificent snifter forgotten in his hand.

"How did you ever figure out that Estella didn't commit the murders. After Dender's statement the entire case seemed as clear as glass."

DeKok smiled and raised his glass.

"Take a sip first and tell me if this is not an excellent cognac."

Vledder took a sip, joining the other. His eyes lit up. It *was* an excellent cognac. Because of his close association with DeKok, the young man had developed a real fondness for the double-distilled wine. But soon he was impatient again.

"Come on, DeKok, give."

"It wasn't all as simple as it seemed," relented DeKok. "There were too many inconsistencies."

"Such as?"

DeKok took another sip and looked at him over the brim of his glass. Then he continued.

"Such as Red Bakker. He did not fit in at all. He never was a patient of Dr. Beaumonde and he didn't figure at all in the tale of the tall, skinny man. And yet Red Bakker died by the same hand that killed Jan-Willem Hoffman and Alex Peetersen. Please note, a murderer who was an expert shot. When I took a closer look at that, I suspected that Estella could not have been the shootist. There was no reason to believe she ever even handled a gun."

Vledder reacted vehemently.

---

* Vledder is currently a Commissaris, in line for promotion to Chief-Commissaris. He's a highly respected police officer, not at all like some of the superiors depicted in Baantjer's books. Some people think Vledder will make Chief Constable before retirement. *(translator)*

196

"But that was just a suspicion. And Frederick Dender saw her with his own eyes. He was a witness when Peetersen was killed."

DeKok nodded agreeably.

"I never doubted the sincerity of Dender's statements," he said calmly. "Dender was convinced that Estella was responsible for the murders. It was this conviction that persuaded him to kill her. And he convinced the other ex-patients as well."

"A terrible mistake," sighed Prins.

"Yes, it was." DeKok paused. "I wonder if we did right," he added.

"What? Did what right?"

"The unmasking of Felix Beaumonde . . . in the presence of Dender. It was a psychological shock to him. But I had to be *sure*, you understand. You see, even though he knew Estella was dead, killed by him and his accomplices, he *still* recognized Felix as Estella. Felix played his part well."

"I was wondering why you wanted him there."

"Yes, I needed Dender to see Felix in the same circumstances. Besides, we could hardly force Felix to dress up that way for a line-up."

"What about Dender?" asked Mrs. DeKok.

"He's not in good shape. For the time being he has been checked into St. Lucas Hospital. I visited him there. He turned his head away from me. He refused to look at me, not that I blame him. But gradually he changed. He was concerned about the welfare of the other ten, his accomplices. When I left he held my hand. 'If the death penalty still existed, I would have deserved it,' he said."

There was a long pause. Everybody concentrated on their drinks and the platters were handed around.

"You know," said Riggelink, "that a recent poll of the population showed the majority in favor or re-instituting the death penalty, especially the younger people seem to be in favor. What do you think?"

"I don't agree with the death penalty," said DeKok firmly.

"Why not?"

"There is too much room for mistakes. We don't have infallible cops, or infallible juries, or even infallible judges. Instead of the death penalty, I would suggest a life imprisonment without parole. Some people think that's worse, I know, but at least it leaves the door open for a reversal of the verdict if additional evidence comes to light. Once the State has engaged in murder, the verdict is irreversible . . . even if the condemned person later turns out to be innocent. No, the death penalty is too final a solution for us, fallible people."

Vledder had heard DeKok's argument before and did not pay attention. In his mind he contemplated the scene in the dunes along the coast and suddenly he broke the silence.

"But," he protested, "I *still* don't know why you thought that Estella was innocent."

DeKok sipped from his second glass of cognac.

"Well," he sighed. "as I said, because the wounds of the victims indicated that the killer was an excellent shot. That . . . and the murder of Red Bakker. On the day he was fished out of the river, I had a conversation with his girlfriend, Black Judy, and she told me that Red Bakker was figuring on a big haul. Little Lowee confirmed that in a round-about way. Apparently Red had taken pictures of a man in woman's clothing."

"A transvestite."

DeKok ignored the remark and raised a finger in the air.

"If," he said in his most didactic tone of voice, "the killer murders Red Bakker because he made pictures of a transvestite, then a transvestite must play a role in the affair."

Vledder was full of admiration.

"Brilliant . . . simply brilliant," he laughed.

"When I pursued that line of reasoning," DeKok went on, "a conclusion was obvious. If Frederick Dender had seen a woman kill Alex Peetersen, than the killer was not a woman, but a man dressed as a woman."

DeKok ate some of the delicacies his wife had heaped on his plate. He chewed with obvious pleasure.

"Go on," urged his wife.

"I can't eat any faster than this," he said.

"Don't be obtuse, my dear, continue with your story."

"Of course. Well, the thought of a transvestite occupied me. I suddenly realized why the pseudo-Estella always insisted on quiet, remote meeting places. The chance of discovery was less. A precaution, in other words."

DeKok placed his plate on the table next to him and sipped from his glass.

"Felix Beaumonde dictated a complete confession this afternoon. He told me that the idea of blackmail came to him when he found the keys to his father's old safe. At first it was just boredom that made him listen to the tapes. From the start he made it appear as if the blackmail originated with his stepmother. He wrote letters in her name and presented himself at the pay-offs in woman's clothing. That was easy to do, for him. The ex-patients never knew Estella and as long as he could present himself in the guise of a transvestite, he ran few risks. Besides, everybody was *convinced* that Estella was the blackmailer."

"A nasty little man," commented Mrs. DeKok.

"Yes. Felix told me that he consciously put Estella in the position she was in. If something went wrong, she would be blamed. He had a grudge against his stepmother. Estella was the first to detect some homosexual tendencies in her stepson and she discussed it with her husband. Untypically, perhaps, but Dr. Beaumonde was very upset about that. One would expect more understanding from a psychiatrist. But then," said DeKok philosophically, "they're only people too and when their own child is involved, it becomes difficult to remain objective. Whatever the reason, the relationship between father and son cooled."

"Well, was he a transvestite, or a homosexual?"

"A little of both, I guess. In any case a confused young man. Transvestites are not necessarily homosexual and homosexuals are not necessarily transvestites. I think he dressed as a woman, at first, in order to fool his victims. Later he liked it for his own reasons."

DeKok drained his glass and placed it next to his empty plate.

"The truly sad thing is, of course, that Estella was killed for something she was no part of, for something of which she was completely innocent. I don't think she ever realized the reason for her execution."

A long pause ensued. DeKok poured again. Bert Riggelink had the next question.

"What I don't understand," he said, twirling his moustache, "is why Felix came to the parking lot at all? I mean, how did he know about the appointment . . . with, eh, with *me*?"

DeKok leaned comfortably back in his chair.

"Well, I better confess. Let me advise you to confess as little as possible. But I promised to tell you and you certainly deserve an answer."

"It won't go outside this room," assured Bower heatedly. The others nodded agreement.

"Well, after Black Judy's story I had a burning desire to know why Red Bakker thought that *this* particular transvestite was willing to pay big money to keep his predilection a secret. After all, this is Amsterdam! How did Red know the photos were worth money? Who had tipped him off? The more I thought about it, the more I felt that Red Bakker was a key figure in the entire affair. What was his method? I had Henkie inform me about that. After all, Henkie is related to Red in some way. It soon became clear that Red usually gained his blackmail material from the circles of the so-called beautiful boys . . . the gigolos."

Vledder suddenly sat up straight.

"Estella saw those guys, used to hang out with them."

"Indeed. She even provided a room for one of them, a Robby Vanderwal. He could come and go as he pleased. Felix was unaware that the house harbored a second inhabitant. Estella did not discuss her private life with him. But Felix visited the house regularly, of course. That was his base of operations . . . his father's study. Estella was often away and Felix felt completely safe. And that's how it happened that Robby Vanderwal discovered that Felix liked to dress up as a woman."

Vledder nodded his understanding.

"And Robby told Red Bakker and Bakker tried to blackmail Felix."

DeKok smiled.

"Of course, Red Bakker did not know the background. Probably all he knew was that Felix had a lot of money. Red Bakker took a chance. He gambled that he had found a pigeon. I'm sure he was pleasantly surprised when Felix was ready to pay a small fortune for the pictures."

Riggelink rose and went over to the sideboard. As he filled his plate, he grinned to himself.

"Now I still don't know how that appointment came about," he said, sitting down with a full plate.

DeKok rubbed the bridge of his nose with a little finger.

"I arranged a murder. Entrapment, if you will. I knew it would be extremely difficult, almost impossible, to get solid evidence against Felix. I had to persuade him to strike again."

They hung on his words.

"How?" asked Vledder.

"I ... eh, I," hesitated DeKok, "I sought out Robby Vanderwal and put pressure on him. I dictated a letter, a letter to Felix."

"What sort of letter?"

DeKok took a large swallow from his cognac.

"I wrote ... caused him to write, that he, Robby Vanderwal, had gained possession of the photos originally owned by Red Bakker and that he knew about the background of the murders. I also made him write that he had several times been approached by a certain Inspector DeKok from Warmoes Street. He Robby, I made him write, had so far been able to remain silent, but he feared that eventually he would give in to the pressure from the Inspector. That's why he wanted to escape across the border. As initial compensation, Robby thought that an even hundred thousand would probably be needed. The money could be delivered any time, any place, at Felix's convenience ... as long as it was done soon."

"A trap."

"Yes, I sent Robby to stay with relatives in Rotterdam and used an address at Brewers Canal as a return address. I know the doorman of the apartment building. Yesterday morning I received Felix's answer, complete with a street map of Amsterdam. At least the mail is reliable."

"Sneaky," commented Mrs. DeKok.

"Perhaps, but I wanted absolute certainty that Felix would respond to Robby's letter. Before I mailed the letter, I visited Felix in his house at the coast. He lives in a nice villa, paid for by the blood money he extorted from his victims. I expressed my sorrow about the passing of his stepmother and told him, confidentially, that I was about to arrest the killer because I had found a young gigolo who knew more than he was telling. One of Estella's former boyfriends."

Fred Prins grinned.

"Sneaky seems an understatement, almost slimy."

DeKok looked up, not at all offended.

"Murder and blackmail are slimy crimes."

They fell silent, each occupied with his own thoughts. Mrs. DeKok urged them to partake of the delicacies she had prepared and left to make coffee in the kitchen.

When she returned with a large tray with coffee, milk, sugar and enough cups, Bower hastily offered his assistance. Soon, the aroma of fresh-made coffee mingled with the perfume of cognac and the conversation became more general, less tense.

Late that night, after the company had left, DeKok sank back in his favorite chair, a last glass of cognac in his hand. He held the amber liquid up to the light.

"I think I'll be going to bed early for a few nights," he said reflectively. "It's been rather late the last few days. Also, I've the feeling I'm getting too old for this business."

His wife sat down on the arm of the chair next to him and stroked his gray hair. There was a fond smile on her face when she reassured him.

"Not you, Jurriaan, you'll always be young."

About the Author:

Albert Cornelis Baantjer (BAANTJER) first appeared on the American literary scene in September, 1992 with "DeKok and Murder on the Menu". He was a member of the Amsterdam Municipal Police force for more than 38 years and for more than 25 years he worked Homicide out of the ancient police station at 48 Warmoes Street, on the edge of Amsterdam's Red Light District. The average tenure of an officer in "the busiest police station of Europe" is about five years. Baantjer stayed until his retirement.

His appeal in the United States has been instantaneous and praise for his work has been universal. "If there could be another Maigret-like police detective, he might well be Detective-Inspector DeKok of the Amsterdam police," according to *Bruce Cassiday* of the International Association of Crime Writers. "It's easy to understand the appeal of Amsterdam police detective DeKok," writes *Charles Solomon* of the Los Angeles Times. Baantjer has been described as "a Dutch Conan Doyle" (Publishers Weekly) and has been called "a new major voice in crime fiction in America" (*Ray B. Browne*, CLUES: A Journal of Detection).

Perhaps part of the appeal is because much of Baantjer's fiction is based on real-life (or death) situations encountered during his long police career. He writes with the authority of an expert and with the compassion of a person who has seen too much suffering. He's been there.

The critics and the public have been quick to appreciate the charm and the allure of Baantjer's work. Seven "DeKok's" have been used by the (Dutch) Reader's Digest in their series of condensed books (called "Best Books" in Holland). In his native Holland, with a population of less than 15 million people, Baantjer has sold more than 5 million books and according to the Netherlands Library Information Service, a Baantjer/DeKok is checked out of a library more than 700,000 times per year.

A sampling of American reviews suggests that Baantjer may become as popular in English as he is already in Dutch.

Also From InterContinental Publishing:

VENGEANCE: Prelude to Saddam's War
by Bob Mendes

Shocking revelations concerning his past move Michel Moreels, a Belgian industrial agent and consultant, to go to work for the Israeli Mossad. His assignment is to infiltrate a clandestine arms project designed to transform Iraq into a major international military power. Together with his girlfriend, Anna Steiner, he travels to Baghdad and succeeds in winning the trust of Colonel Saddiq Qazzaz, an officer of the *Mukhabarat*, the dreaded Iraqi Secret Police. At the risk of his own life and that of Anna, he penetrates the network of the illegal international arms trade, traditionally based in Brussels and the French-speaking part of Belgium. He meets American scientist Gerald Bull, a ballistic expert. Gradually it becomes clear to Michel that neither Bull, nor Anna, are what they appear to be. The more he learns about international secret services and the people who are determined to manipulate him, the more his Iraqi mission takes on a personal character: one of Vengeance!

A "faction-thriller" based on actual events in Iraq and Western Europe.
A Bertelsmann (Europe) Book Club Selection.
First American edition of this European Best-Seller.

ISBN 1-881164-71-3 **($9.95)**

Bob Mendes is the winner of the (1993) "Gouden Strop" (Golden Noose). The "Golden Noose" is an annual award given to the best thriller or crime/spy novel published in the Dutch language. "An intelligent and convincing intrigue in fast tempo; in writing *Vengeance*, Bob Mendes has produced a thriller of international allure." **(From the Jury's report for the Golden Noose, 1993)** . . . Compelling and well-documented—Believable—a tremendously exciting thriller—a powerful visual ability—compelling, tension-filled and extremely well written—rivetting action and finely detailed characters—smooth transition from fact to fiction and back again . . . **(a sampling of Dutch and Flemish reviews)**.

ALSO FROM INTERCONTINENTAL PUBLISHING:

TENERIFE! (ISBN 1-881164-51-9 / $7.95) by Elsinck: A swiftly paced, hard-hitting story. Not for the squeamish. But nevertheless, a compelling read, written in the short take technique of a hard-sell TV commercial with whole scenes viewed in one- and two-second shots, and no pauses to catch the breath (*Bruce Cassiday*, **International Association of Crime Writers**); A fascinating work combining suspense and the study of a troubled mind to tell a story that compels the reader to continue reading (*Mac Rutherford*, **Lucky Books**); This first effort by Elsinck gives testimony to the popularity of his subsequent books. This contemporary thriller pulls no punches. A nail-biter, full of European suspense (**The Book Reader**).*

MURDER BY FAX (ISBN 1-881164-52-7 / $7.95) by Elsinck: Elsinck has created a technical tour-de-force. This high-tech version of the epistolary novel succeeds as the faxed messages quickly prove capable of providing plot, clues and characterization (**Publishers Weekly**); This novel by Dutch author Elsinck is so interestingly written it might be read for its creative style alone. It is sharp and concise and one easily becomes involved enough to read it in one sitting. MURDER BY FAX cannot help but have its American readers fall under the spell of this highly original author (*Paulette Kozick*, **West Coast Review of Books**); This clever and breezy thriller is a fun exercise. Elsinck's spirit of inventiveness keeps you guessing up to the satisfying end (*Timothy Hunter*, **[Cleveland] Plain Dealer**); The use of modern technology is nothing new, but Dutch writer Elsinck takes it one step further (*Peter Handel*, **San Francisco Chronicle**).

CONFESSION OF A HIRED KILLER (ISBN 1-881164-53-5 / $8.95) by Elsinck: Elsinck saves a nice surprise, despite its wild farrago of murder and assorted intrigue (**Kirkus Reviews**); Reading Elsinck is like peeling an onion. Once you have pulled away one layer, you'll find an even more intriguing scenario. (*Paulette Kozick*, **Rapport**) Elsinck remains a valuable asset to the thriller genre. He is original, writes in a lively style and researches his material with painstaking care (*de Volkskrant*, **Amsterdam**).

* Contains graphic descriptions of explicit sex and violence.

Murder in Amsterdam
Baantjer

The two very first "DeKok" stories for the first time in a single volume, containing *DeKok and the Sunday Strangler* and *DeKok and the Corpse on Christmas Eve.*

First American edition of these European
Best-Sellers in a single volume.

ISBN 1 881164 00 4

From critical reviews of **Murder in Amsterdam**:

If there could be another Maigret-like police detective, he might well be Detective-Inspector DeKok of the Amsterdam police. Similarities to Simenon abound in any critical judgement of Baantjer's work (*Bruce Cassiday*, **International Association of Crime Writers**); The two novellas make an irresistible case for the popularity of the Dutch author. DeKok's maverick personality certainly makes him a compassionate judge of other outsiders and an astute analyst of antisocial behavior (*Marilyn Stasio*, **The New York Times Book Review**); Both stories are very easy to take (**Kirkus Reviews**); Inspector DeKok is part Columbo, part Clouseau, part genius, and part imp. Baantjer has managed to create a figure hapless and honorable, bozoesque and brilliant, but most importantly, a body for whom the reader finds compassion (*Steven Rosen*, **West Coast Review of Books**); Readers of this book will understand why the author is so popular in Holland. His DeKok is a complex, fascinating individual (*Ray Browne*, **CLUES: A Journal of Detection**); This first translation of Baantjer's work into English supports the mystery writer's reputation in his native Holland as a Dutch Conan Doyle. His knowledge of esoterica rivals that of Holmes, but Baantjer wisely uses such trivia infrequently, his main interests clearly being detective work, characterization and moral complexity (**Publishers Weekly**);

DEADLY DREAMS
by Gerald A. Schiller

It was happening again ... the mist ... struggling to find her way. Then ... the images ... grotesque, distorted figures under plastic sheeting, and white-coated, masked figures moving toward her ...

When Denise Burton's recurring nightmares suddenly begin to take shape in reality, she is forced to begin a search ... a search to discover the truth behind these horrific dreams.

The search will lead her into a series of dangerous encounters ... in a desert ghost-town, within the restricted laboratories of Marikem, the chemical company where she works, with a brutal drug dealer and with a lover who is not what he seems.

A riveting thriller.

ISBN 1-881164-81-0
$9.95

A thriller of fear and retaliation, *Gary Phillips,* **author of Perdition, USA**; ... promising gambits .. a *Twilight Zone* appetizer, **Kirkus Reviews**; ... a brisk, dialogue-driven story of nasty goings-on and cover-ups in the labs of a giant chemical works with a perky, attractive, imperiled heroine, *Charles Champlin* [Los Angeles Times].